The Calf of

All the Masai people
exception. Of all
November Cloud wa
day to own her. Wh
raiders and the Novem
on a dangerous adventure to rescue her.

The Calf of the November Cloud is an exciting story of life on the great plains of Africa, of the ways of its people and how they live with the cruelty of that beautiful land – with drought and hunger, and the terrible floodwaters of the monsoon rains. It's also a tale of the special relationship that can grow up between a human and a wild animal, when Konyek is helped by that most powerful and intelligent of creatures, the elephant.

"There are so many things to recommend in this book that it is difficult to know where to begin." **BOOK WINDOW**

"An absorbing story written by someone who loves Africa and has an intimate knowledge of Kenya and its native people." **JUNIOR BOOKSHELF**

Also by Hilary Ruben in Piper

Beyond the Bamboo Fence

Hilary Ruben

The Calf of the November Cloud

PIPER
PAN MACMILLAN CHILDREN'S BOOKS

First published 1977 by William Collins Sons & Co Ltd
This Piper edition published 1993 by
PAN MACMILLAN CHILDREN'S BOOKS
a division of Pan Macmillan Ltd
Cavaye Place London SW10 9PG and Basingstoke
Associated companies throughout the world

1 3 5 7 9 8 6 4 2

ISBN 0-330-33205-8

Printed and bound in Great Britain by
Cox & Wyman Ltd, Reading, Berks.

This is the story of a Masai boy, and his love of a special calf in his father's herd. The Masai are nomads, and they live in *manyattas*. A *manyatta* is a circle of huts which look rather like elongated igloos, made of twigs and plastered with cattle dung and mud. The huts are surrounded by a protective barrier of interwoven thorn-tree branches, and at night the cattle are herded into the centre of this circle.

The adventures of Konyek are of course imaginary, but the Masai customs and traditions, myths and stories introduced are authentic. So, too, is the Masai love of their cattle in general, and their passion for a favourite animal in the herd in particular.

Authentic as well are the habits of the two elephants who help Konyek, and it is not beyond the bounds of possibility that two real elephants might behave as they did. Many strange stories are told in Africa of these animals, of their intelligence and their gentleness and their strength, some of them no stranger than this story.

The little ones are just like children; yet today their parents are being killed in their thousands by poachers greedy for ivory. With no one to look after them, and teach them, and love them, these orphans may die. Many of the wild animals with whom we share this beautiful earth are today in danger, and they will only be saved if each and every one of us cares deeply enough. Even thinking about them with caring.

H.R.

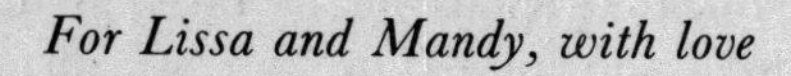

For Lissa and Mandy, with love

CONTENTS

1

A Calf is Born

Just before dawn, at the hour when the buffalo go to drink, Konyek awoke and slipped outside his little home of mud and twigs. The stars were still bright and hard, and he could make out the circle of snug dwellings and the cattle in their midst. He could hear the wind in the branches of the thorn trees, and he could hear the low growling of a lion. But he did not feel afraid, for the oblong huts of mud and wattle of the manyatta were encircled by a high barricade of twigs.

He moved amongst the cattle, and even in the dark he recognized the shape of each one, patted its warm flanks, and called it softly by its name. Suddenly the wind blew a moon like a silver bubble across the sky, and it shone down on the circle of huts, and on the cattle in their centre, and on the slender form of the boy. Then, in its ashen light, Konyek saw the form of a calf that had just been born. With a cry he knelt by its side, and, caressing its wet coat, he talked to it gently. He could see that it was the colour of ebony, and that on its forehead there was a mark like a summer cloud.

The sun rose round and red in the pale sky; it grew redder and hotter until it seemed to set the sky aflame, and now all the manyatta was awake. The women came out to milk the cows, and the herdsboys made ready to take the cattle to pasture. Only Konyek made no move, remaining by the side of the newborn calf. At length his father approached, and he said:

"It is well. The cow of the Lesser Rains has given birth at last."

"Yes, my father," Konyek replied. "She gave birth in the night, before the hour when the buffalo go to drink. See how beautiful her calf is – what are you going to call it?"

And his father thought for a moment, and glanced at the sky, and then he answered:

"Now is the month of November, when the clouds in the heavens turn white. Look at the horizon, my son, look at the clouds fat as goats after the rain of the Pleiades, and white as their kids. Let us call her the Calf of the November Cloud, because that was the time of her birth, and because there is a mark on her forehead which is like a small white cloud."

And so the calf was named, and Konyek was satisfied. It became his favourite, and he longed only to prove his courage, so that one day his father might give it to him for his own.

2

A Time of Plenty

In the days that followed, Konyek's heart was full of gladness, because of the calf, because of the water that laughed in the river, and because the grass was golden and tall. Each day he took his father's cattle to pasture, and always he stayed close to the side of the calf of the November Cloud. He liked the soft warmth of her flanks, and the velvety softness of her black neck, and he liked to keep special watch over her so that she came to no harm. For amongst the wild animals that roamed the hills and the plains, there were leopard, and hyena and lion.

He was not afraid himself. He knew that the animals would not threaten him unless he threatened them, and that they only killed when they were hungry. The scents in the air, the footprints on the earth, and the droppings of the animals on the ground told him which of the game was close at hand; and from a long distance away, his sharp eyes could make out their forms. Even the tips of their ears he could recognize when they showed above the long grass. From the circling vultures he knew that lions were feeding on a kill, and that the birds were waiting to pick at the bones. When the rain bird began its monotonous call, he knew that the clouds would soon gather, and the heavens pour water upon the thirsty earth. When the honey-bird sang out, he knew that if he pursued it, it would lead him to a tree where the bees swarmed, and stored their combs of honey. Where the white egret flocked, there were elephant, for the egrets followed in their wake, eating the insects unearthed by the heavy tread of their huge feet.

Sometimes his younger brother Marangu accompanied him, and sometimes he went alone, roaming the plains and the hills where the wild fig grew, and the slender fever trees with their tiny leaves and needle-like thorns. Bright birds darted from their branches – starlings with sea-blue wings, and lilac-breasted rollers, and golden weavers.

Sometimes Konyek would meet his cousin Parmet herding the cattle. Formerly they had gone out together, and been glad of one another's company, for they were like brothers. They lived in the same manyatta, and the mother of one was a mother to the other, so that every child had many mothers and fathers, and many grandparents also. But lately, Parmet had changed. He had grown loud and boastful, and he avoided Konyek's eye because he was jealous of him. He saw that Konyek was the favourite of their grandfather Ol-Poruo, who was famous throughout the land for his wisdom and for his bravery. He saw, too, that the girls favoured

Konyek with their glances, and the boys listened to his words. But Parmet was stronger and older, and he competed with his cousin by a show of words, and a display of strength, so that sometimes the others were afraid of him.

During this time of plenty, Konyek did not think about Parmet. He watched the herds of zebra and buffalo, he watched the graceful impala with their finely wrought horns, he watched the baboons grooming one another, and he watched the calf of the November Cloud grow strong on its mother's milk.

When dusk fell, he returned to the manyatta. The circle of huts blended with the earth, for they were of the same colour, just as a mole or a hedgehog is the same colour as the earth. Their frames were of interwoven twigs, and these frames were plastered with cattle dung to keep them waterproof in the months of the rain. There were neither doors nor windows, only a small, low opening, and all the corners were curved, so that their shape was a little like the shape of a cowrie shell. And the entrance was narrow and dark like a small tunnel which curved into a little room of earth and twigs. It was lit by the flames of the fire, and Konyek felt safe and snug here; the rounded corners were full of shadows, the rounded calabashes that stood upon the floor were full of milk, and his brothers and sisters were all about him. In the light of the yellow flames which flickered in their circle of stones on the earth floor, he could see his mother's smiling face, and the layers of beaded necklaces that she wore, and the long strips of beaded cowhide that hung from her ears.

Now came the hour of talking, and this was the hour that Konyek loved best, for it was the time that his grandmother, the wife of Ol-Poruo, told her stories. She told how the world began, she told about the first Masai, and she told of the cunning of the animals; she told, too, of men who were sometimes wicked and sometimes brave. On this night, during the time of plenty when the calf of the November Cloud was two moons old, Konyek asked her to tell the story of the children of the sycamore tree.

His grandmother smiled, and there was a light in her faded eyes like the fire when it burns low, and her face was lined as the earth when it awaits the rain. The children crept close about her, the flames flickered, and it was quiet, and warm, and safe; then she began her story.

3

The Children of the Sycamore Tree

Many years ago, there lived a woman who was no longer young, and she lived alone. God had not blessed her either with children or with a husband, and she was unhappy, although she did not understand the reason for her distress. But one night she dreamed that her hut was full of children: there was the sound of their chattering and the joyfulness of their laughter, and there was the warmth of their embraces. Then she awoke, and the hut was silent and empty. Now she knew why she was troubled, and she said to herself: "I am unhappy because I live alone, and because I have no children. Therefore I will go to the witch-doctor who lives at the foot of the Hill of Wise Decisions, and I will ask him for his help."

She milked her cow and tethered it so that it would not stray too far away. Then she set off for the home of the witch-doctor, leading a goat by a cord of plaited grass. She followed a narrow path that the elephant had made through the close-growing bushes and the bamboo until she came to a stream. Fluffy-coated water buck with large, soft eyes were drinking, and chestnut impala, and a cow elephant with her calf. The water of the stream was bright and clear, and the woman stooped to drink also. As she bent down, she caught sight of her reflection in the water, and she saw that it was neither young nor beautiful, and she was yet more troubled than before. But she put her faith in the witch-doctor, and hurried on with the goat.

At last she caught sight of a hill with a high cone-shaped summit, like a tall straw hat; up here, a long time ago, the elders of the village had judged some bad men, and because they had judged wisely, and well, the people had named the place the Hill of Wise Decisions. At the foot of this hill there was a circle of huts, and here the witch-doctor dwelt.

He was sitting on a cowhide beneath a sacred fig tree, just outside the manyatta, and beside him was his gourd full of magic stones. He was very old, and his eyes were full of the knowledge that he had inherited from his father and his grandfather before him. The woman said to him:

"Oh witch-doctor, I have the trouble!"

And the witch-doctor said: "The trouble of what?"

And the woman said: "Behold, I am no longer young, and I have neither husband nor children."

The witch-doctor thought for a few moments, and then he asked: "Which is it you want? The husband or the children?"

And the woman thought to herself: "I would like

both, but if he sees that I am greedy, perhaps he will not give me either. If I choose a husband, he may beat me, and he may send me away from him because I am too old to bear him any children."

And so she answered: "I do not wish the husband. I wish the children."

And the witch-doctor said: "Go look for the cooking pots, and pick up as many as you have the strength to carry, and take them to a fruit-bearing sycamore tree. Go early in the morning, at the hour the sun decorates the sky, and pick the fruit of the sycamore tree, and fill the pots with them. Then return to your hut, and put the pots inside, and go for a long walk, and do not return until the hour that the cattle return to the manyatta."

The woman thanked the witch-doctor then, and gave him the goat she had brought as a gift, and said: "Well, I am about to go."

And the witch-doctor replied in the manner of the Masai: "So be it. Good-bye. Pray to God, approach only the things which are safe, and meet nobody but blind people."

Whereupon the woman answered in the manner of the Masai: "Lie down with honey-wine and milk."

And the witch-doctor, nodding his wise grey head, replied: "So be it."

Then the woman departed, returning along the elephant trail to her hut. When she arrived home, the moon had already risen, and she saw that it was full; so she milked her cow, and tipped a little of the milk on to the ground, saying to herself: "God likes this. I will have the children, and they will grow safely, even as the moon has grown safely to its full size this night."

Then she went into her hut and slept. And in the morning, at the hour when the sky is the colour of smoke, she gathered together her cooking pots, and borrowed one more from her sister, and went to the place where there was a fruit-bearing sycamore tree. Now it was the blood-red time, the time when the rising sun inflames the sky, and in accordance with the commands of the witch-doctor, she picked the fruit of the sycamore tree and filled all the pots. After this, she took them to her hut, and, leaving them inside as the old man had bid her, went for a long walk. When she grew tired, she lay down beneath a fig tree and slept. It was midday when she awoke, the hour when the sun stands, and she waited till the shadows lowered themselves, then started on her way home.

As she drew near, she heard the voices of children at play. She stood still, listening incredulously, and said to herself: "How is it that I can hear children playing in the house?" And she went inside then, and found that her house was full of children. All her work was done; the girls were sweeping the floor, the boys had taken her two cows and her goats to graze, and the warriors were dancing outside in the manyatta.

So now she was happy, because she had many children, and she remained with her children for many days.

But it came to pass that one day she scolded them,

saying: "You are but children of the sycamore tree." Whereupon the children fell silent and did not speak, and when she had gone out of her hut into the manyatta, they slipped away and returned to the sycamore tree. Then they disappeared, becoming again its fruit as before.

The woman returned to her hut, and discovered they were not there, not even one, and she wept all night long. In the morning, when they had not come, she set out once more for the home of the witch-doctor. Once more she followed the path made by the elephants, and crossed the stream where the impala and the bush-buck and all the animals went to drink, then continued on her way until she came to the Hill of Wise Decisions. The witch-doctor was sitting outside his hut, and she said to him:

"What have you done now? The children that you gave me, they have gone."

And the witch-doctor said: "Now I do not know what you should do."

And the woman asked: "Shall I go look again amongst the leaves of the sycamore tree?"

And the witch-doctor replied: "Go, try."

The woman returned then to her hut, and in the morning, at the time when the sky is the colour of smoke, she collected together all her pots, and borrowed one from her sister as well. Her sister's children woke up, and asked her where their cousins had gone the day before, and whether they had returned. But she had no words, only tears, and could not answer them.

She went with the pots to the sycamore tree and climbed into its branches as before. But behold! The eyes of the fruits came out to stare at her, and she was so frightened she could not move.

All day long she remained in the tree, and the gaze of the eyes did not waver, and her limbs remained rigid with fear. But just before the hour of darkness, two young warriors happened to pass nearby. She called out to them, and they helped her down, and accompanied her back to the manyatta. Never again did she search for the children, but her hut was silent and empty, and often she wept long into the night; even many years afterwards there were times when she cried.

The children were quiet when their grandmother finished the story. A twig crackled in the fire, and outside they could hear the high humming of cicadas. After a while the old woman said to Konyek:

"Why were the children taken away from the woman, my son?"

And he answered without hesitation: "Because she was ungrateful, and did not appreciate what she had received; therefore God punished her."

Parmet looked at Konyek, his eyes dark with jealousy because his cousin had answered wisely, and because their grandmother favoured him. She nodded her head approvingly, night wrapped itself closely about the hut, and the children slept. Only Konyek lay awake on the stretched skins, disturbed by his cousin's glance and Parmet's hatred for him. Slipping outside, he called softly to the November Calf which was standing with the rest of the herd in the middle of the circle of huts. It recognized his voice, and came over to him. Throwing an arm about its neck, Konyek gazed up at the gleaming summit of Kilimanjaro, the mountain of his people and the dwelling place of their God. Its rounded dome seemed to sit upon a cloud like a silver pearl; gazing at it, he forgot about his cousin and grew calm. Later, when he slept, he dreamed that he was a silver bird, and that his nest was a star that hung above the mountain.

4

The Beginning of the Thin Time

The months passed, the land lost its cloak of green and gold and turned dusty and brown. Now all the grass on the plain in front of the manyatta, and all the grass on the hills behind, was eaten down until no more remained. And now, as well, the water ceased to laugh in the river, and that part which flowed past the manyatta dried up first. These were the hungry months, the thin ones, and Konyek wandered far from home, the November Calf always close beside him, in search of pastures.

Sometimes he saw his cousin Parmet not far away, and when their gazes met, Parmet's eyes were resentful and sullen. When they were children they had played together and shared each other's secrets; but now Parmet spoke no words to his cousin, and Konyek began to fear that the other boy might, in his spite, do some harm to the calf of the November Cloud.

April came, and the sky was stabbed with lightning. Konyek knew then that the great bird of the heavens was beating the water with its wings, and that the silver flash in the sky was the silver shine of the water. But it did not rain. The red god roared angrily, and the black god rumbled its answer, but still it did not rain. Each afternoon, at the hour when the shadows lower themselves, clouds gathered and they were as a dark frown in the sky; each afternoon, a little later, the sun dismissed the clouds, and no rain came.

May passed, which is the last month of the year for the Masai, and the people waited for the change of the weather which often comes with the full moon; but the moon waxed and waned and there was no change. Twice more it waxed full and round, twice more it diminished to a tiny scar on the face of the heavens, and still the sun continued to burn the earth as before.

Now the grass was short and white as stubble in a field of harvested corn, and the streams were all running dry, so that Konyek was forced to roam further than ever in search of water and pasture for his father's cattle. He began to be afraid, and most of all he feared for the calf of the November Cloud. In times of drought, the cattle began to die, and the first to die were the calves, for their mothers' milk dried up, like the rivers and the ponds and the marshes. The calf of the November Cloud was weaned now, but she did not have the strength of a full-grown animal to withstand the hunger that was upon the land. When he returned to the manyatta at dusk, Konyek prayed to God for rain, singing with the other boys and girls of the manyatta:

"Fall, rain, fall,
Take the dry skin of the earth
And my thirst;
Fall, rain, fall,
Take the earth's rough hide away,
Bring us milk and grass today."

And the old men of the manyatta, who were as his grandfathers, burnt a special wood called cordia wood, and into the flames they threw a charm given them by a witch-doctor. Then they gathered round the fire and sang the hymn of the old men:

"The black god, ho!" one called out alone.

And the others replied in chorus:

"God, to whom we pray,
Water us this day."

And the one man called out alone again:

"The black god, ho!"

And the others shouted in chorus:

"GO, DROUGHT, GO!
God, God, to whom we pray,
Water, water us this day."

The women sang their hymn, too, and fastened grass to the hems of their skirts. And when still the rain did not fall, Ol-Poruo, who had foreseen the drought in his dreams, spoke with the other old men, the Elders, and it was decided that they should visit the witch-doctor. They took two goats as a gift for him, and a calabash of honey-beer; then they departed.

Konyek watched them go, and then he too left the manyatta and went with the cattle to look for grass. As he walked by the side of the November

Calf, he saw that she had grown thin; and now her mother gave little milk, and he knew that soon the people and the animals would be hungry. Already his stomach felt a little empty. He put his arm over the neck of the calf, and drew comfort from the warm softness of her body. Ngai, the God of his people, would help; the witch-doctor would use his power and intervene on the part of the people, and soon there would be rain. But he could not wait for it to come. This very day he must find water for his cattle, and he swore softly to the November Calf that she would slake her thirst before nightfall.

He kept to the valley, for that is where the water that has gathered from the hills remains when the rest of the land grows parched; he did not notice that his cousin was following. He noticed only that the stream had run dry, and upon its bed there was nothing but stones. He followed its course further than he had ever followed it before, past large rocks and overhanging bamboo; but still he found no water.

He left the river bank and went out into the broad valley. Now he saw many different sorts of animals all mixed together, drinking: the zebra and the gazelle, the buffalo and the baboon, the hyena and the giraffe. Already some were leaving, and by the time he arrived with his cattle nothing remained but thick mud.

Now he did not know in which direction to turn. Everywhere there was the fierce heat of the sun, and there was the smell of the dust, and there was the thirst of the cattle, the thirst of the November

Calf especially. In his desperation, Konyek turned towards the mountain, and, gazing at the dazzling whiteness of its summit, stretched out his arms in a prayer.

When he turned his eyes to the valley again, he saw in the distance a small figure. The man was running, and in his hand he carried a bow and arrow. He paused for a moment, and then ran on again, and at the same time Konyek heard the call of the honey-bird. By this he knew that the man was a Dorobo, and that he was pursuing the bird who would lead him to honey. Now Konyek left the cattle and ran after the Dorobo, thinking to ask him if he knew where there was water. For the Dorobo are wanderers without homes, hunters of elephant and eaters of honey; and they know the secrets of the land as the animals know them, and the birds.

Swiftly Konyek followed him, and, hidden in the bushes, Parmet watched. He watched his cousin leave the dry bed of the stream and run swiftly along the slope of a hill where yellow cassias were in blossom, and the scarlet flame tree also. When the honey-bird settled in a cassia where the bees were swarming, Parmet watched Konyek catch up with the Dorobo.

The hunter had not seen or heard Parmet, for he was too far away even for his sharp ears and quick eyes. But he knew that Konyek was there even before he turned his head; he had heard the sound of his feet tapping on the earth like the faint beat of a drum long before he reached him, and he had smelt the scent of him in the air.

"How are the cattle?" the Dorobo asked, for he was familiar with the Masai people, and the manner in which they sometimes greeted one another. And Konyek answered:

"The Elders are gone to the witch-doctor, that he might make rain, and the earth bring forth the life-giving grass."

The hunter nodded, and seemed to forget the boy. He twirled a stick that the Masai call the male between his two hands, and bored it into a flat piece of wood that they call the female, until he created a spark. Then he lit some dry grass from the sparks, and put it beneath some dung, which he had placed in the bark of the tree. Konyek waited patiently the while, for it would have been impolite to ask immediately the thing that he wished to know.

"Soon, the smoke will drive the bees away," the hunter said. "Wait a while, and I will share the honey with you, and we will leave a little for the bird; or she will curse me for my ungratefulness."

Now Konyek was hungry, and he loved the sweet taste of the honey, and it was not often that he was offered it. But he would not wait, because his anxiety for the cattle was even greater than his desire for the honey. So he thanked the little man, whose legs were thin and bent as the branches of a whistling thorn, and whose eyes were small and bright as a bird's, and he said:

"Oh, you the hunter, you who are so wise in the way of animals and birds, have you seen any water in all your wanderings?"

And the Dorobo replied: "There is a pool not far from here that the elephant have made with their mighty feet, in the manner of elephant when there is drought. Go there, and see. Perhaps the water has not all dried up."

Then he told Konyek how to find the pool, and Konyek thanked him again, and ran back to his cattle.

He drove them in the direction that the hunter had told him, over the ridge of the hills and into a neighbouring valley; and he did not notice that his cousin Parmet was following. He looked only ahead of him, anxiously scanning the land for a glimpse of water. Then he caught sight of a small herd of elephant, and indeed the animals were drinking just as the Dorobo had said. He waited for them to finish, and his impatience was great; but at last they wandered away, and he approached with his cattle. He went ahead with the calf of the November Cloud, who approached when he called her name, and remained close by his side in the manner of a dog. He let her drink first, in case the remaining cows might muddy the water, and such was his anxiety for his cattle that he forgot his own thirst. Then he saw his cousin approaching with his uncle's herd; but Parmet was too late, for Konyek's own cows had already drunk and the water was muddy. The two boys exchanged no word, but Konyek could feel his cousin's hatred for him.

Just then, Konyek's sharp eyes caught sight of a movement in the bushes where the foot of the hills met the valley. He stood very still, and watched closely. In a few moments he saw that it was a lion; and that the lion was making ready for a kill.

It moved slowly, its steps were full of purpose and its energy restrained. It was moving towards his cattle, and Konyek shouted to Parmet; but his cousin made no response. The lion continued to prowl towards the herd, its yellow eyes intent upon its prey. Now Konyek was gripped by a terror so great it squeezed the breath from his body. The lion continued to approach, and Konyek stepped in front of the November Calf to protect it. Nearer it came, and yet nearer, and Konyek felt the wild beating of his heart. The cattle stood motionless as though their fear had turned them to stone. Now the lion was no more than thirty yards away, and it seemed that its eyes were fixed on the November Calf. Konyek forgot everything except the calf, and he began to run towards the lion, screaming and waving his stick in an attempt to scare it off. But the lion sprinted forward towards him.

At that moment, an arrow sped through the air. It pierced the heart of the lion: the animal faltered, and fell upon the ground. Konyek knew then that his friend the hunter was near, and had shot the arrow and saved him.

The little Dorobo approached, and, looking at him with eyes that were kind and bright in his wizened face, gave him honeycombs.

"Take these," he said. "Eat of their sweetness in this time of hunger." And before Konyek was able to thank him for saving him from the lion, he departed as swiftly as he had come.

Konyek tasted the honey and it was good; but he kept it to share with his brothers and sisters. When he returned, they ate of it gladly, for they were hungry. He told them then about the Dorobo who had given it to him, and how the little hunter had saved him from the lion. But of Parmet's cowardice he said nothing. For he and Parmet belonged to the same age-group and were therefore as brothers, and Parmet would have been mocked by all the boys and girls of their age-group had they heard how he ignored Konyek's cry for help. Konyek held no grudge in his heart against his cousin, and he was rewarded with praise for his own bravery. He prayed that his father would remember, and that when he was circumcised, and became a man, he would give him the calf of the November Cloud for his own.

In the evening when they sat round the fire, the children were hungry, and to take their thoughts from their hunger, their grandmother told them the story of the first Dorobo.

5

The First Dorobo

In the beginning, before God had created the cows and the buffaloes, the forests and the mountains, there were only three living creatures throughout all the land. One was an elephant, another a serpent, and the third a Dorobo. Then God created a cow, and the Dorobo took it and became a herdsman. And the animals and the man all lived together.

The man grew attached to the cow, but he disliked the serpent, because whenever the snake breathed upon him, his body began to itch; and one day he asked why this was. And the serpent answered: "Oh my father, I do not wish to offend you with my breath, you must forgive me."

The Dorobo made no answer, but in his heart he did not forgive him, and that night he struck the serpent on the head with his club, and killed it. In the morning, the elephant missed his small friend, and he said to the Dorobo:

"Where has the thin one gone?"

The Dorobo replied that he did not know, but the elephant, with his wisdom, knew what the man had done, and that he did not wish to admit his guilt. There was nothing he could do, for his friend was dead, and he remained silent.

Night came, and the rain fell, and there was grass for the Dorobo's cow, and water for it to drink. And in time, the elephant gave birth to a calf, which she watched over tenderly. The months passed, and the calf grew strong on its mother's milk, but there was no more rain and the grass had withered and the streams had run dry. Only one small pool remained, and after the elephant had eaten, she would go there to drink, then lie in the water to cool her skin. For this reason, when the Dorobo arrived with his cow the water was muddy, and he said to himself: "If I kill the elephant, she will not wallow in the pool, and my cow will be able to quench her thirst when the day is ended. But the elephant is much bigger than I am; how can I possibly hope to rid myself of her?" Thus it came to pass he invented the bow and arrow, and shot the elephant with the arrow, and killed her.

The young elephant was sad and lonely now, and she said to herself: "I do not wish to remain here any longer with the Dorobo, for he is bad. He killed the snake, and he killed my mother, and I shall go away and live some place else."

For many days and many nights she wandered across the land, until she came to a place where there were trees, and grass, and water. There was plenty to eat, and plenty to drink, and she stayed.

One day she met a Masai, and the Masai asked her whence she had come, and she replied: "I have come from the home of the Dorobo who lives far away in the forest. He killed the snake, and he killed my mother, and so I went away from him, and came to live here."

This news interested the Masai, for he had never seen a Dorobo, and he asked the elephant to take him to the place where the man lived. The elephant agreed, and the two of them set off together.

At last they arrived at the home of the Dorobo, and the Masai examined it curiously, for it was made of dried grass, and looked to him like a great bird's nest facing skywards. The Dorobo did not see the Masai for he was inside his house; but just then God called the Dorobo, saying:

"Come thither tomorrow morning at daybreak, for there is something I wish to say to you."

But the Masai also heard the words of God, and in the morning he rose before the Dorobo, and stood high on a hill-top, and cried out to God, "Behold, I have come!"

Then God told him to take an axe, and to build a large manyatta, which must be completed in three days. Then he must go and search in the forest for a thin calf, which God had hidden amongst the trees. Then, when he had found it, he must carry it back to the manyatta, and kill it, and strip off its hide, and tie the meat inside. But he must not eat the meat, and he must tie the hide outside the door of his hut. Then he must cut much wood, and light a big fire, and throw the meat into the flames. After this, he must hide in the hut, and soon he would hear a great noise outside that was like the crashing of thunder; but he need feel neither alarm nor astonishment.

All this the Masai did. He went into the forest, and searched there until he found the calf. Then he took it back to the manyatta, and slaughtered it, and stripped it of its hide, and tied the flesh inside. Then he cut wood, and lit a great fire, and tossed the meat into it; and last of all he went into the hut and hid himself as God had commanded. There he waited, and when at last he heard a mighty roaring that was like the crashing of thunder, he remembered God's reassurance, and was neither alarmed nor astonished.

He was hidden in the hut, and could not see the cause of the uproar, but God had commanded that a long strip of hide should hang down from heaven, and that the tip of the hide should reach just above the cowhide. Then he caused cattle to descend the leather thong; one by one they came down from heaven until at last all the manyatta was full of cattle, and they were crowded one against the other, and finally they broke down the hut in which the Masai was hiding. And he forgot God's words and cried out: "Oh! Oh!" in alarm and astonishment.

Then he went outside the hut. But the strip of hide had been severed, and no more cows were coming down from heaven. And God said:

"Are there enough cattle? You doubted my powers, and you were lacking in faith, and alarm and astonishment overcame you. Therefore neither this day nor any other day will I send you more cows. These are all that you will receive."

The Masai returned home with the cattle which

God had given him instead of the Dorobo; and he tended them well, and their numbers multiplied. But the Dorobo, who lost the cattle because of the Masai's cunning, has had to hunt for his food ever since, and shoot with his bow and arrow.

Thus it came about that because, in the beginning the Dorobo had only one cow and God gave cattle to the Masai, the Masai believe that all the herds of the land belong to them. And when they see cows in the possession of other tribes, they think that they have been stolen. Therefore they say: "Let us take them, for they belong to us. Did not God give us all the cattle he created when first he put them upon the earth?"

The children smiled, pleased to think that all the cattle on the earth belonged to their people. But Konyek thought of his friend, the little hunter, and felt sorry for the Dorobo who must shoot elephant for meat because they had no cows' milk to drink.

He lay down beside his brothers and sisters to sleep. A hooded eagle hooted in a thorn tree, and the moon slipped in and out of the wind-tossed clouds.

Suddenly there was a great clap of thunder, followed by another, and the children awoke, and some of them thought that it was God sending down more cattle to earth. But the older ones recognized the sound and listened eagerly for the patter of rain. Ol-Poruo went outside, and watched the lightning's steely brilliance flare across the sky; and he too listened and waited.

But no rain fell.

6

The Attack

Now the thirst drove the animals together in great throngs: elephant, zebra, gazelle, buffalo, giraffe and rhinoceros intermingled in the great trek for water and for nourishing grass. They pressed onwards together in their terrible search, the dust rising in a red cloud behind them, and some of them died on the way. Already Konyek had seen the first carcass of an elephant, and the small form of a baby zebra. In the days that followed he saw many more, for it was nature's way of thinning the numbers of the animals when they had multiplied too greatly.

He saw, too, the first dead cow-calves, and he feared for his father's herd, and for the calf of the November Cloud especially. Then his grandfather, Ol-Poruo of the Unconquered Shield, called the people together, saying:

"The time of the dry month is at hand, the month when the small birds follow the cattle, and the earth waits for the rain. But the sky is not yet ready to water the earth, the great bird of heaven does not beat the water with her wings, nor the black god grumble behind the clouds. Yet there is no more grass on the earth near our manyatta than there are hairs on the palm of my hand. Therefore, let us wait a while, and if no rain comes, we will move on and find new pastures for our cattle." And the people heard his words gladly, and murmured their assent.

That day, Konyek returned to the pool that the Dorobo had shown him. He saw a few elephants were there, and that three of them were digging with their great forefeet, and had reached water. Now they waited for the mud to settle, controlling the calves that wished to rush forward to satisfy their thirst. While he waited, he watched baby baboons riding on their mothers' backs, and timid lizards darting silently across the rocks where he sat. The sun seeped deep into the thirsty earth, and it was still, and bright, and hot.

The elephants finished drinking, a little water remained, and again he waited for the mud to settle; then he went forward with his cattle. When they too had drunk, all the water was finished, and there remained only the mud at the bottom. Now it was that Konyek saw Parmet approaching, and he knew that his cousin would bear him ill will because there was no water left for his cattle.

There were a few dried stalks of grass nearby, and for some time the two boys let their herds graze close to one another, but not a single word passed between them. Konyek saw that his cousin's glance was resentful and sullen, and he could feel Parmet's jealousy burn him as he felt the rays of the sun. So he decided to move away, but just as he was about to drive the cattle before him, a terrible shrieking shattered the stillness, and he felt his blood grow chill as mountain water.

He recognized the sound even before he saw the flash of spears and the band of warriors come racing towards him, uttering their blood-curdling cries. His head was giddy with fear, and he tried to drive the cattle before him, and to make them disperse amongst the bushes. But already the warriors were almost upon him, and he flung his arms around the neck of the November Calf as though at least she alone he would save. Then the gleam of a spear dazzled his eyes, and he felt a scorching pain in his right shoulder; then a sickening black wave swept over him, and he fell to the ground unconscious.

Meanwhile, Parmet had run with all speed to hide in the bushes. Peeping through the leaves, shaking with fear, he had seen the spear strike his cousin, and he had seen him fall to the ground. Now he watched the raiders drive a number of the cattle before them and make off across the range of hills that bordered the other side of the valley. When they were out of sight, he herded the cattle that belonged to Konyek's father, together with his own, and, pausing only to glance at his cousin, set out for home.

He knew that Konyek must bleed to death on the sun-baked earth, but in his heart he felt no pity. He thought only of the way in which he would win the admiration of his age-group with the story that he

was already inventing, and how with cunning words he would become the favourite of Ol-Poruo, and how his father and mother would praise him as well.

When he was back at the manyatta, he told the people of the raid, saying: "I had found water, and Konyek followed me. Then, after he had watered the cattle, he went into the shade with his favourite calf, and whilst he was lying asleep with his head on its flanks, the raiders suddenly came. On hearing their terrible cries, he ran off into the bushes to hide, but I remained with the cattle, and with his cattle also, for I had been watching them while he lay sleeping in the shade. I could not protect them from the warriors, and I shouted to Konyek, but he had run away and hidden himself. The warriors did not harm me, but they took some of the cattle of my uncle. All the rest I brought back with my own. I called Konyek, but he did not come, and I searched for him, but I did not see him. Nor could I delay, because our warriors must be told of the raid, so that they might retrieve the cattle. Therefore I returned without my cousin."

Now everyone praised Parmet for his behaviour, and he accepted the praise modestly. Only Ol-Poruo was sparing with his words, for he could see into Parmet's heart, and he knew of his deceitfulness. But Konyek's father and mother did not know, and they were ashamed, for they believed that their son had run away like a coward, and that he had neglected the cattle as well.

But there was little time to think of any of this now; already Ol-Poruo had sent word to the warriors to come to him with all haste. They lived in another manyatta, together with the young men who were training for their warriorhood, and with the young girls. The manyatta was not far away, and soon they appeared with their spears and their shields. When they were all assembled, the old men poured milk and honey-wine on to the ground saying, "God wishes it," and the women sprinkled the warriors with milk from a gourd, which was as a blessing. Then the warriors set off. They knew which direction to go, for Parmet had told them, and they knew as well to which tribe and clan the raiders belonged, for he had described the markings on their shields. Soon they picked up their trail and followed it in a long, silent line, each man in his given place according to the markings on his shield. Swiftly they moved, with set faces and purposeful steps.

Konyek's father set out, too, in search of his son, and Marangu, who had begged to accompany him, went with him. Anxiously Konyek's mother watched them depart across the plain, until their figures became quite small. His grandparents watched as well, and all that day their old eyes returned to the plain. But when at last Marangu reappeared with his father, Konyek was not with them.

The next day, Parmet's mother and sisters and Konyek's mother and sisters went to the manyatta of the warriors to wait for them. They went very early, and they tied grass on their skirts, and they took gourds of milk with them saying:

"Our children will soon be returning, and when they arrive, they may be hungry."

And before the morning star had disappeared, they prayed to God, singing:

"God to whom we prayed for children
Return our children to us safely
Return our children to us, we beg thee."

And they watched, and they waited, and at the hour when the shadows begin to lower themselves, one of the women gave a shout, for she had sighted the warriors, and they were returning with the cattle. All of them had been retrieved, and only one calf was missing, which was the calf of the November Cloud.

Then the people knew that Parmet had been speaking the truth, for he had said that Konyek had left the herd and gone into the shade to sleep, and that he had rested there with his head on the flanks of the calf. When Ol-Poruo heard, his heart was heavy. But the boys and girls of Konyek's age-group were full of scorn for him, because he had acted in the manner of a coward, and because he had neglected his father's cattle.

In Konyek's firelit home that evening, the children were quiet, for Konyek was gentle and patient with them, and they missed him; and the warm contentment of the room was disturbed by wisps of sadness which drifted from the hearts of the people, mingling with the shadows and flickering with the flames. In the morning they were going away, and if Konyek had not returned, they would not be able to wait for him, for the cattle were thirsty and hungry, and the water and the grass were gone.

7

The Little Hunter

At the time that the raiders carried off the cattle, the Dorobo hunter was following the honey-bird. It flew from tree to tree, calling to the hunter, and waiting perched upon a branch until he caught up with it. In this fashion he came to the valley where he had first seen the elephants digging for water with their feet; and he smelt the smell of the cattle, and he saw the fresh droppings upon the earth, and he knew that a herd had passed just recently. Then, although it was far away, with his sharp eyes he saw a form lying upon the ground. He began to run towards it, and the honey-bird called and called, but he did not return, nor even pause to look back. For even from the distance he knew that the form was Konyek's.

He found him still unconscious where he had fallen, and weak with loss of blood. Gently he lifted him up and carried him across the valley to the foot of the range of hills. Here he cut a shelter within a thick clump of bushes, and made a bed of branches and laid Konyek upon it. Then he hurried away to look for certain roots, and the bark of the cassia tree. When he returned, he made fire, and when the twigs he had cut were burning, he poured a little of his precious water from a gourd, and boiled the roots of the plants in it. Then he bathed Konyek's wound and covered it with the healing leaves. Night fell, and he waited anxiously by his side, for he saw that the boy was very sick.

Not until the next day did Konyek regain consciousness, and all this time the little hunter remained close by, neither moving nor taking his gaze from him. As soon as the boy opened his eyes, he gave him water to drink in which the bark of the cassia tree had been boiled, for this would help the fever. And then he took a strip of the precious bark of tall podo tree that he carried in his leather bag, and this too he boiled in water, for it would help relieve the pain.

For two more days the fever raged, and Konyek did not know where he was, or what had happened to him, and the hunter cared for him tirelessly, tending the wound with his medicine.

On the afternoon of the second day, an old man passed through the sun-dazed valley. The Dorobo ran after him, thinking he might be from Konyek's manyatta, in which case he could take back news of the boy to his family. Besides, the hunter desired to know as well all that had taken place there in the valley, and it was likely that the old man knew, for news travelled quickly from mouth to mouth.

The Elder was not from Konyek's manyatta, but he dwelt nearby, and he had indeed heard the whole story. He told it to the Dorobo, and he told him, too, how all the cattle had been retrieved, with the exception of one calf with a mark like a white cloud upon its forehead. But this calf, he added, was the one that Konyek had taken with him when he slept in the shade of the bushes.

Now in his mind the hunter questioned Parmet's story, for he had seen himself how Konyek had stayed with the cattle when the lion attacked, and he had seen, too, how he searched far and wide to find water for them. But he did not discuss this matter with the Elder, and only told him that the boy had been gravely wounded, and that he was still unconscious. Then he pointed out the place where he was lying, and asked the old man to take this news to his family, explaining that he could not leave the boy in order to deliver the message himself. The old man promised, and went his way along the heat-filled valley; and the hunter returned to the cool refuge he had made in the bushes.

In the morning, the fire began to leave Konyek's body, and the pain to lessen, whereupon he remembered all that had happened. For the first time, too, he recognized the face of the little hunter, anxiously bending over him as gently he tended his wounds. Then he cried out:

"Where are the cattle? Has the enemy stolen them all?"

And the hunter answered him: "No. Not all. But even those that were stolen your warriors have already retrieved. It is three days now that you have been lying here sick and sorely wounded. You lost much blood, and for a while I feared for your life." He hesitated, and then continued: "Yesterday I spoke with an old man down there in the valley. He told me all that had passed, for his manyatta is not far distant from yours. He told me that only the black calf with the white mark on its forehead had not been retrieved, for Parmet your kinsman said that this calf was with you."

Konyek frowned, and the hunter watched him carefully. "The November Calf was with me, and I was with the herd. I do not understand the words of my cousin. What other news did the old man tell you thither in the valley?"

Then the Dorobo repeated all of the man's words, and he saw the boy's eyes begin to glint fiercely as a leopard's when it is angered; and indeed a great rage was burning within Konyek, although it was a rage that came to him seldom, for usually he was calm and quiet. In this, and many other things, although he did not know it, he was like his grandfather, Ol-Poruo.

Then he told the hunter that Parmet had been lying, and that his cousin had left him in the valley to die because of his hatred for him. And the Dorobo gazed at him quietly, and knew that the boy was speaking the truth.

Konyek remained silent, but he was not brooding upon his cousin's treachery, for all his thoughts were flying to the black calf which had not been retrieved. And he determined to go and search for her the moment he regained his strength.

He knew that he should not set out on this quest without permission from his father, but he feared his father might refuse; at the same time he knew he would be unable to rest until the calf had been found. Therefore he was torn between his love for it, and his obedience to his father, for obedience to their elders, and respect for them, were matters which his people treated with great seriousness.

He tossed and turned restlessly, troubled by his thoughts, and he was restless, too, because of the anger that smouldered within him against his cousin Parmet. And it seemed to him that if he could regain the calf, and thereby prove his courage, it might help him to regain favour in the eyes of his family, for he had no means of disproving Parmet's words.

The hunter slipped away to shoot game for food, and Konyek stayed restlessly in the leafy shelter, watching the valley. It was hot, and dry, and very still. More animals passed, wandering like refugees in their terrible search for food and water, and it occurred to Konyek that the calf of the November Cloud may have died of thirst; and this was why the warriors had failed to retrieve her. But he cast the thought from his mind, and tried to walk a little so that he might regain his strength more quickly, for he was anxious to depart.

The hunter returned, carrying a small gazelle which he stripped of its skin, and then roasted. But Konyek would not eat of the meat, for his people permitted themselves only the flesh of oxen or goats.

Yet only on a feast day did they slaughter an ox, for they loved their herds, and knew each one by name, and could not bear to kill them for food save to mark a special occasion. Instead of meat, they took a little blood from the animal, piercing a vein in its neck with a blocked arrow, and letting the blood drip into a gourd until they had sufficient. Then they stopped the vein with a plug of dung, and they mixed the blood with milk; this was their chief sustenance.

Konyek ate the nuts which the hunter offered him, and he ate as well the roots, which he had not tasted before, and the honey to help restore his strength. The Dorobo, seeing his restlessness, distracted him with stories of Ol-Poruo's bravery in the days when he had been a warrior. And he told him how he had helped to fashion Ol-Poruo's famous shield, and how he had crushed scarlet berries from a certain tree to make the red colour necessary to the design painted upon it. For the Masai never made their own shields, but ordered the Dorobo to do so, paying them with goats and with cattle, and treating them as their servants. They treated the tribe of the El Kuono as servants also, for these people were tinsmiths, and knew how to sift the iron ore from the sand of the river beds, and smelt it, and fashion spears and bracelets. The hunter told of the El Kuono who had carried Ol-Poruo's shield for him into a famous battle, and Konyek's heart filled with pride as he listened to the accounts of his grandfather's courage. Then he remembered how Parmet had disgraced him in the eyes of the great man, and he burned with shame, and resolved to clear himself.

Night came, and the stars the Masai call "the widows" appeared, shining near the three stars they wish to marry (which are called "the three old men"). Then the moon showed herself reluctantly through a faint haze, as though she were trying to hide herself behind the bridal veil she had worn when she married the sun. Konyek had not spoken of the things which troubled him, but now he asked the hunter if he would show him the place whence the raiders had come, so that he could try and retrieve the calf of the November Cloud. And the hunter hesitated, for he expected one of Konyek's kinsmen to arrive from the manyatta at any moment and he knew that the boy should not depart without his father's permission. But he knew, too, of Konyek's love for the calf, and he wanted to help him.

"Let us wait until the hour when the sun adorns the sky," he said. "Let us sleep first, and make a decision when we wake."

Konyek nodded, but he was impatient, and could not rest. The hours passed slowly, and he walked a little in the moonlit valley, for now his strength was returning quickly. Then he returned to the leafy shelter and lay down on the bed of branches that the hunter had prepared for him. But the thoughts continued to turn in his head like leaves eddying in a gust of wind.

The hunter slept lightly. Even in his sleep he was aware of the sound of the wind in the branches, or the distant trumpeting of an elephant; and now he was aware of Konyek's restlessness. A hyena cackled, and its mad laughter echoed in the valley, and he said to the boy, for the sound had woken him fully:

"The hyena is no longer young, and a lion is chasing him."

"No," Konyek said. "He is still young, and he has found a wife and is making love to her."

"It is true," the hunter said. "When a hyena laughs, he is young and full of joy; or he is old and full of fear, and no man can tell the difference."

"Look," Konyek said. "The moon is hiding her face. Is the rain coming?"

"After the moon is full, the rain will come. Do you not know that in the beginning, after the sun and the moon were married, they quarrelled, and struck one another? And because the sun was ashamed, and did not wish the people to know he had been fighting, nor allow them to see his bruises, he hid behind the clouds, and sulked. And while the rain was falling he made up his mind to shine so brightly, no man would be able to look upon him without half closing his eyes. But the moon was less perturbed, and even appeared with a piece bitten out of her cheek, and continued to shine soft and pale as before."

The hunter's voice trailed off into silence, and he slept once more. For a while, Konyek listened to the creaking complaints of the bushbabies in the fig tree, and the high, small cries of the fruit-bats. Then at last he too slept.

When he awoke, day was breaking, and seeing

that the hunter was already up, he said, "In a little while, the sun will stain the sky blood-red. Have you decided yet?"

And as no one had come from the manyatta, the hunter replied, "Yes, I have decided. I will help you."

"It is good," Konyek said. "My strength has returned. Let us depart immediately." And so they set out along the valley.

8

The People Move On

The people of Konyek's manyatta were also departing, for there was neither water nor grass for the cattle. His mother carried calabashes out of her home, and cowhides, and cups that were made from the horns of the buffalo, and loaded them on to the donkey. She took her beaded jewellery and a few goatskins as well, and all this time she kept looking across the plain at the foot of the manyatta to see if Konyek was coming. But the plain was empty.

Now there came to the manyatta Konyek's older brothers and cousins who belonged to the group of the Fearless Ones. These were the warriors, and the younger men amongst them who were training for warriorhood, and they came with the young girls with whom they lived in another manyatta not far away. In twos and threes they came; the men were tall and finely built, and very proud, and the girls were slender and smiling. The spears of the warriors shone in the sun, and their hair fell in finely-twisted strands to their shoulders, and it was covered in a paint made from the red earth, which they call ochre. Parmet gazed at them, longing for the time when he would become a man (which was not far off now), and go to live with the warriors and the young girls.

He was glad when at last Ol-Poruo picked up his knobbed stick, and his fly switch, and his spokesman's club of rhinoceros horn, and at last they were ready to leave. For he, too, had been looking across the plains, fearing that if Konyek were still alive he might return to the manyatta and reveal that he, Parmet, had lied and deceived. But when they set off and still Konyek did not come, his mind was at rest for he was certain that his cousin must be dead.

Ol-Poruo and Marangu and his mother and father hung back, and continued to gaze across the plain, until the sun climbed the hill behind the manyatta; then, sorrowfully, they too departed, following the small clusters of people with their cattle and their goats and their donkeys.

The young men and women walked ahead; they walked lightly and with ease through the sunlight and the wind. All the men wore sarongs, all the women skirts of goatskin, and because they owned so little they moved freely across their wide, high, land. Nourished by the milk they had drunk before their departure and accustomed to walking long distances, they did not grow tired; only the very old and the very young amongst them became weary from the journey and the heat of the sun. So they stopped at midday and rested beneath slender trees with tiny leaves and thorns like needles. Giraffes looked down on them with the dreamy gaze of sleep-walkers, and wrapping long tongues around the leaves, continued their feeding.

Marangu lay on the grass, and his eyes were on the giraffes, but his thoughts were with his brother Konyek. He watched the golden weaver birds that flew in and out of their round nests hanging from the branches, and he watched the great white clouds, but still his thoughts were with his brother Konyek. Then his gaze rested on the gleaming dome of Kilimanjaro, his people's mountain, and his grandmother said:

"Know you that in the beginning the sky married the earth, and made love to her as a man makes love to a woman. And just as a woman bears children after a man makes love to her, so the earth bore grass and flowers; and it gave birth as well to Kilimanjaro, the mountain, which is the dwelling place of our God."

The heat of the sun lessened, and they moved on. The little children sat on the donkeys amongst the cowhides and the gourds, and the mothers and the little girls carried the babies on their backs. Parmet walked with the girls and boys of his age-group, the age-group of the Big Ostrich Feathers. They were as young as twelve years of age, and as old as nineteen, but they did not count their birthdays, for this did not matter to them. Only the age-group to which they belonged was of importance. Parmet was amongst the oldest and strongest, his voice was loudest, and he thirsted for praise and admiration. He had resented Konyek because he was the most popular amongst the young girls, and because the youths had preferred his company also. But now his cousin was no longer there to attract them with his quiet strength (which all his own boastfulness could not command), and so they paid him greater attention. At first he lay awake at night, remembering how he had left Konyek to die of his wound on the plain; but soon he forgot about him.

The sun disintegrated in the sky and dusted the earth with a film of gold, and the people halted by a narrow stream. The water that trickled through it was clear and cold, and they stooped to drink, and the cattle drank as well. The women filled their gourds, and milked the cows; but their udders were almost dry and it was necessary to leave something for the calves. The men twirled sticks between the palms of their hands and made fire, for with the darkness came the cold; and Marangu and his brothers and sisters gathered round the fire with their grandmother. The smallest ones cried a little, because they were hungry, and there were those amongst them who cried for Konyek, because he was patient with them, and gentle. His grandmother missed him, too, for he was her favourite, and in the clouds that drifted across the moon, it seemed to her that she could see his face. Then Marangu tugged her gently by her arm, saying:

"You are sad because you are thinking of Konyek."

And she answered him: "Yes, my thoughts follow the boy even as the leaves follow the current of a stream. And I await the rain, for the earth is dry as the bones of a wildebeest a month after the vultures have cleaned the last scrap of flesh from them."

"It is the fault of the red god," Marangu replied. "Tell us the story of the rain gods, my grandmother, it is a long time since we have heard it."

"Yes," the children echoed, "it is a long time. Tell us the story, Grandmother, tell us!"

The woman nodded her head, which was shaved in the manner of married Masai women, and, smiling her wise old smile, began:

One day, the black god who is good said to the red god who is bad, "See, the people are dying of hunger. Let us take pity on them and give them some water." And the red god agreed, and the black god caused dark clouds to gather over the earth, and there fell much rain. Then the red god commanded the black god to stop the rain, because the people had had sufficient; but the black god disagreed, and the rain continued. The red god sulked, and they did not speak to one another until the black god agreed to stop the water. But the earth was still dry and the grass was neither plentiful nor green, and so the two gods began to argue again. And the red god said he would kill the people because the black god was spoiling them, and the black god said: "I shall not allow my people to be harmed. I live close by them, and you live above me, therefore I am able to protect them."

He fulfilled his promise, and the people were not harmed, and even today he continues to watch over them. For when the clouds gather and the thunder crashes above them, it is the red god threatening to kill the people; but when in the distance there is a low rumbling, it is the black god saying, "Leave them be; do not harm my people. I shall protect them."

And even as she ceased speaking there was a flash of lightning which lit the hills and the thorn trees with its bright white light, followed by a distant rumble of thunder. Again Ol-Poruo looked at the moon, and again he thought that soon the rain would come, but there was only the wind in the cassia trees and the cicadas' high hum. Then he and all the people fell asleep beneath the stars.

At sunrise the following morning they started on their way again. Late that afternoon, before the hour when the cattle return to the manyatta, they came to a hilly place where pine trees grew, and the eucalyptus, and the wild fig; and it was agreed amongst Ol-Poruo and the Elders that there they should stay. One more night they slept beneath the stars, then in the morning the womenfolk began to build their new homes.

Laughing and chattering like a flock of weaver birds making their nests, they wove branches into frameworks, and plastered them with cattle dung through which the rain could not seep. Inside, they made partitions of *leleshwa* stems, so that there were three rooms: a long narrow one for the goats, a small one for the mother and her youngest baby, and a large one where all the family gathered. In this room, next to one of the walls, they made a low platform of branches which they covered with cowhides, and this was for the children to sleep upon; it was the place where visitors would sit as well.

By evening, when all was ready, a wind blew up. Leaves swirled in the air, and it was very dark. Then there came a mighty crash of thunder, followed by another, and yet one more.

And then, at last, the rain began to fall.

It beat on the dry, hard earth like a drum, it beat in the hearts of the people like a joyous song. Now there would be water for their cattle, now the blessed grass would sprout once more, and now milk would flow from the udders of the cows.

Ol-Poruo shared his people's joy, but his thoughts turned often to Konyek, and there was disappointment in his heart, because the boy had failed him; and he had expected him to follow in his footsteps.

Parmet, too, thought of him, and there was triumph in his heart because now he was the leader of his age-group, of the Big Ostrich Feathers, and because Konyek had failed Ol-Poruo of the Unconquered Shield, and he need never feel jealous of him again.

9

Konyek Begins His Search

During all this time, Konyek had gone far away from the manyatta. All of the first day he had walked with the little hunter, even though his wound hurt him, and he was soon exhausted because he had not yet fully recovered his strength. At last they had come to a place where the land rolled gently, like a great park, and there were tall trees, podo, and cedar, and the smaller wild olive. There had been a little rain, but it was still dry, the earth beneath their feet hard as baked clay, the grass bleached and stubbly as a field of threshed corn. Now they were near the village whence the raiders had come, and they were no longer in the territory of the Masai. The hunter had found a sheltered place beneath the wide branches of a cedar tree, and while they were sitting by the fire, watching the stars, Konyek said:

"You have saved my life, and I shall never forget what you have done. But I must retrieve the calf alone. It is my quarrel, and they are my enemies.

Besides, am I such a coward that I cannot fight the herdsboy and take back the calf without help? This I must do myself. So in the morning, depart and go your way. And one day, come to the manyatta of my father that I might know your news, and that my father might give you some gift in repayment for all that you have done."

The hunter looked at him with little eyes that were bright with cunning and kindness, and he said:

"Had the grandson of Ol-Poruo of the Unconquered Shield come to harm, I should have been grieved. If I have saved his life, then I am joyous. What other gift delights the heart of a man more than gladness such as this? I desire no repayment, but one day I will go to the manyatta in order to find out whether you have returned safely with the black calf. Also because I wish to know the judgement of the Elders after they have listened to your words, and the words spoken by your cousin Parmet."

"I shall not return to the manyatta without the calf of the November Cloud," Konyek said. "I must find her because of my love for her, and I must find her that I might prove my courage to my people. Only by this means can I hope that my father will forgive my disobedience, and the Elders know that Parmet's story of my cowardice was a lie."

The hunter nodded, and gazed through the branches of the tree at the stars. Soon he and the boy slept, lying close to the fire for warmth.

In the night, the hunter was awakened by a far-off

ound that was like small waves breaking on a listant shore. He knew that it was the drum of a Dorobo trying to tell him something, and he sat up, and remained very still, and listened very attentively. He concentrated with all his mind to know what he drum was trying to tell him, for the message of a lrum is received in the same way that one person ar from another sometimes receives a thought. The lrum ceased, and the hunter knew that it was elling him that his kinsmen were in trouble, and he nust go to their help.

He sat quietly for a few moments, his gaze on the leeping boy. He did not wish to leave him, for he ad intended to remain in the vicinity in case Konyek should fall into danger. But now he knew hat he must go. Picking up his bow and arrow, his eather pouch and his gourd, he slipped into the ight, noiseless and shy as a bush-buck. Later Konyek woke, and found that he was gone. But he ad left him the little store of honey and nuts he had athered to sustain them on their journey.

Konyek felt very much alone, for he had grown ccustomed to the companionship of the little unter, and he had come to feel a safety in his resence, although he had not realized this at the ime. Yet in a way, he was glad that he was forced o continue by himself, and thus to test his courage.

He set out in an easterly direction, as the Dorobo ad told him, towards the village of the raiders. Now he forgot that he was alone, for it was the hour when the cattle leave the manyatta, and at any noment he might meet with a herd. And amongst them he might see the calf of the November Cloud.

It was raining a little, but rays of early sunlight slipped through the frayed clouds; then a rainbow appeared, which the Masai call "father's garment." And looking at it, Konyek thought that if his brother Marangu had been with him, Marangu would have said in the manner of Masai children: "I will give it to father, because he will like it." But then the rainbow disappeared, and Konyek was glad, for its appearance whilst the rain was falling meant that soon the rain would cease.

Just then, he saw a herd of cattle approaching. Quickly he concealed himself in a tree, and waited. The cows came nearer, and soon he could see their colours quite clearly, and that one of the calves was black. His heart began to beat more quickly. A boy was leading them, and Konyek looked at him carefully, and saw that he was taller than himself. And he saw as well that he was not a Masai, but of a different tribe. Konyek kept his eyes fixed on the black calf, but soon he saw that her lines were not quite similar to the lines of the calf of the November Cloud; and nor was there a white blaze on her forehead. He waited until the cattle were quite far away, and fighting to overcome his disappointment, continued on until he came to a low range of hills. Climbing to the top of the ridge, he saw the village of the raiders.

It was all just as the Dorobo had described. The huts were near the stream at the foot of the hill, and on the other side of the stream there was a steeply wooded escarpment, whose summit was crowned with boulders. All the cattle had already gone out to pasture, and now he must wait until dusk, and the hour of their return. He decided to descend into the valley and to cross the river, and to hide in the forest on the other side.

The stream was full of water from the rain. The water rushed round boulders smooth as ivory, and bubbled over green and brown stones. In the forest there were touracos with scarlet wings; and there were monkeys, and bushbabies, and red-billed storks with wide grey wings. There were trees he had never seen before with green lichen wrapped thickly around their branches, and fungus like old men's beards, and vines that hung down like ropes.

All day long he explored the forest, which was very old and full of secrets. For a million years trees had been growing in this place, and the thick undergrowth hid many animals and millions of insects. Startled bush-buck and little duikers fled for cover, and once a short-sighted rhinoceros trotted past him.

He came to a lake which lay at the foot of a circular crater and climbed down to the water's edge. Here he rested for a while, for he was still not strong, and ate of the honey and the nuts that the hunter had left him. Two elephants went into the water to drink, and he watched them spray their backs with their trunks, then feed on the grass by the lake edge. They came very close to him, and he could see their little eyes, which seemed to him full of kindness and wisdom.

Above all the wild animals he liked the elephant,

because of their gentleness, and because they helped one another in a way that the other animals did not. If one of the herd fell sick, and lay down, two others would prop it up, and help it to walk. If one of them injured its trunk so that it could not pull the leaves from the branches or the grass from the earth, another would feed it. And when one of them died, others would sometimes throw grass and branches over it, then later return, and carry away the bones, and hide them in the bushes.

Now the two elephants were so close he could have touched them, and he talked to them as he talked to the cattle, and there was no feeling of fear, neither he of them, nor they of him.

When they began to climb out of the crater, he went with them, marvelling at the fashion in which the creatures pulled their great bulk up the steep incline, and how, when they descended the escarpment later, they slid down on their bottoms like children. But now the hour when the cattle return to the manyatta was approaching, and he forgot the elephants, and took up a position in the forest opposite the village. From here he could see without being seen.

He felt the impatience mounting within him, and the fear as well; for if the calf of the November Cloud were not amongst the cattle when they returned, it would probably mean that she had died of hunger or thirst.

He fought his fears, and waited, and soon he saw the cattle silhouetted on the ridge of the hill behind the village. They began to descend towards the huts – grey cows, and brown ones, and piebald and white, their calves amongst them.

And then he saw it. The black calf with the white cloud on its forehead. It had grown very thin, but he could not mistake it; he knew its lines as well as he knew the smile of his mother's face. His heart pounded with excitement. He could hardly restrain himself from racing from his hiding place, and running to meet the calf. Then it disappeared with the other cattle amongst the huts.

It grew darker, and he could see the smoke curling from the huts, and he could hear the tinkling of cow-bells, and the voices of the people. These were familiar sounds, and they made him think with longing of the snug warmth of his own firelit home.

The sound of the voices died away, the people slept, and it occurred to him that perhaps he could slip in amongst the huts and steal the calf away. But he knew that if anyone saw or heard him, he stood no chance of escape, for all the village would be aroused. He knew, too, that the old men slept lightly and little, perhaps only for two or three hours.

The night seemed without end. Finally Konyek could restrain himself no longer, and made his way through the trees back to the river. There was no moon, but the sky was strangely light in the manner that it sometimes is before a storm. A wind had arisen, and he was glad of this, because its sound in the trees was like the rushing waters of a flooded stream, and no one would be able to hear him.

He crossed the river, stepping over the smooth

boulders, then slipped into the village the other side. Almost at once he recognized the form of the calf. But just as he was hurrying towards her, pushing his way through the cattle, there was a brilliant flash of lightning followed by a mighty crash of thunder. Instantly the people of the village awoke. Konyek stood motionless for a moment, not even daring to breathe. Then he raced away from the village.

No one saw him, for by the time they came outside he had already gone.

He went back into the forest and made himself a shelter of branches to protect himself from the rising storm. The wind thrashed the branches of the trees, and the great drops of rain turned into a wall of water that joined earth to heaven. Soon the shelter began to leak. When at last day broke, Konyek's limbs were chilled and stiff. He rubbed them, and stretched himself, then returned to the stream so that he could keep watch on the village.

He knew before he arrived there what had happened. He knew by the sound in his ears which was as the sound of a high wind. Yet he was not prepared for the transformation which met his eyes. The stream had trebled in width, and the water, now brown and muddy, swirled past trees which had before stood upon the bank. He knew that if he tried to cross, the current would sweep him away, and that he must wait for the angry water to subside, unless he could find a safer place elsewhere.

Now the village was beginning to waken, and he watched the people come forth from their huts, and gaze at the flooded river which now passed very close to their village. Then the women milked the cows, and soon the herdsboy drove the cattle out of the circle of huts to pasture. It was the same herdsboy as the previous day, but this time he was accompanied by a younger brother.

The calf of the November Cloud appeared last of all, and Konyek could hardly restrain himself from running after her. Anger and longing stormed within him, as the wind had stormed in the forest the night before, and he began to run along the edge of the water, forcing his way through the dense bamboo. On and on he ran, until he saw that it was futile, and there was no place he could cross.

He turned back and walked listlessly through the trees, listening to the roar of the foaming water; and soon he came upon the two elephants that he had met in the crater. They were pulling branches from the trees, and they held each branch on the ground with one great foot whilst with their trunks they delicately stripped off the leaves. He was glad of their company, and remained beside them all that day, talking to them as he talked to his father's cows. Sometimes, when they looked at him with their wise little eyes, it seemed to him that they understood.

When it drew near the hour of dusk, Konyek left the elephants and returned upstream to keep watch opposite the village, so that he might catch a glimpse of the calf of the November Cloud when she returned from pasture. Again he saw her, and again he could not touch her, but must watch helplessly from the other side of the river.

He went back to his shelter, and he was cold and he was hungry. He had almost finished the nuts and the honey the little hunter had left for him, but he put some aside for the morning. In the chill, damp darkness of the forest, he thought of the firelit warmth of his home, of his family seated round the fire in its circle of stones, and of the rounded gourd full of milk upon the floor And he longed with a great longing for his home, and he felt very cut off, and very alone. He tried to make fire, but the wood was too wet, and would not spark. He thought then of the little hunter and missed his company as he missed it so often. Sometimes, in the darkness, he saw the yellow glow of eyes; once he thought he made out the form of a caracal cat, and once a giant forest wart-hog rushed blindly by; but the only animal he feared was the leopard. For it alone might pounce, in the way that a cat pounces upon a mouse, even though it had neither been provoked nor was in need of food. Then he remembered the two elephants, and called them, desirous of their company and hoping they might recognize his voice.

The rain began to fall again. It fell as it had fallen upon the previous night, streaming from the sky in a skein of water that joined heaven to earth. Then he felt a movement of the tree beneath which he had built his shelter, and at first he did not know what it was. Very soon he realized that the two elephants were close by, and that one of them was rubbing itself against the tree-trunk. He greeted them gladly, and they did not leave him.

The hours crept by, and drifting between sleep and wakefulness, he began to have strange dreams. In one he dreamed that he was on a sun-drenched island that floated like a water-lily in the middle of a blue lake. Beside him was a gigantic gourd full of milk, and his grandmother poured some milk from it into a drinking horn, and gave it to him. Then Parmet appeared, leading the November Calf and exclaiming: "Behold, Ol-Poruo has given me this calf because I am strong and brave and have found favour in his eyes!" And when Konyek tried to take the calf it turned into an empty drum, and he awoke, frightened. Soon he fell into a half-sleep again, and this time he dreamed that he was sitting by the fire in the hut at home with his brothers and sisters, and his grandmother was telling them the story of the Children of the Drum.

10

The Woman and the Twins

It happened that once there was an old man, and he had two wives, one of whom bore him many children, and the other who was barren. And one day, the one who bore him many children gave birth to twins, so that there was much rejoicing. Then the wife who was barren said to herself:

"What shall I do to make my husband love me, I who can bear him no children?"

And she went, and she made a small cut in the fingers of the twin boys, and she rubbed the blood on the mouth of their mother while she lay sleeping. Then she said:

"Oh, my people, the woman has eaten her children!"

And they said: "Come, let the men of the manyatta go look."

And they looked, and they saw the blood, and they saw that the children were not there; for the barren wife had hidden them in a drum and thrown them into the river.

And the father of the children said: "What shall I do to this woman who has eaten her children?" And he called her to him and he said to her:

"You ate the children whom you yourself bore. Therefore I will make you work, and you will herd donkeys until the day you die." And so she became the woman who herds the donkeys all her days; and the drum in which the barren wife had put the children was carried by the water to another country.

The old men who were sitting outside their manyatta near the river saw the drum, and one of them said: "That drum there is mine."

And another said: "And that which is inside it is mine."

Then they took it from the water, and opened it, and found the two boys within; and the old man who had claimed the contents of the drum took the children to his home. He reared them until they grew big, and were circumcised, and became warriors. And when their friends met them they called: "How is it with the Children of the Drum?"

And they asked:

"Why is it said to us 'of the Drum'? What is it that happened to us?"

And the people told them, and the twin warriors said to each other: "Let us capture some cattle and go to the country which we came from, and take the cattle as a gift."

And they went on a raid, and captured many cattle. Then they passed through a wood and came to the country where they had been born. And they saw a woman herding donkeys outside a manyatta, and they said to her:

"Why are you herding donkeys? It is the work of children to herd donkeys outside the manyatta."

And the woman answered: "Yes, my children, I will tell you. My husband had two wives, and I bore him children, but the other woman was barren. And then I had twins, and they were both boys, and the other woman cut the fingers of the children, and she picked the children up and put them in a drum and threw it in the river. And she jumped at me, and rubbed the blood on my mouth, and she said to the people of the manyatta: "Come ye, she has finished her children." And the people came, and I said to them that it is a lie, I did not eat them, but they saw the blood the other wife had put on my mouth, and they said it is true, and they gave me the donkeys to herd all of my days."

Then the warriors knew that the woman was their mother, and they said to her: "We are your children. A drum carried us up the river, and other people picked us up, and fed us. And when we grew up they called us 'The Children of the Drum', and we asked them why, and they told us. Behold our fingers." And the woman saw that there were two small scars, and she knew that the warriors were her children. Then they said:

"Come, milk these cows, and leave those donkeys."

And the donkeys wandered into the manyatta and the people said: "Where is the herdswoman?"

And the next day they saw her, and she was

wearing beautiful clothes, and they said: "Ho! What has she got, the herdswoman of the donkeys who formerly ate her children!"

And her husband approached, saying: "I will strike her."

But the warriors said: "Father, leave her alone, do not strike her; go, call the men of the manyatta and we will talk together."

So they came, the men of the manyatta, and they found that the old man was the father of the warriors. And the old man said: "I will strike the barren woman that she may die."

And the warriors said: "Do not strike her, father. Give her the work which formerly you gave to our mother."

And the old man did this, and the woman herded donkeys all the days of her life.

The voice of Konyek's grandmother became the voice of the rain, and the hot sun of his dream was swallowed up by the black chill of the night. He curled himself into a tight ball, and tried to keep warm. He pretended he was a hedgehog, he pretended he was a mongoose in an anthill, and the shivering night dragged on, and on.

11

The Flooded River

At last the sky began to lighten, like the pale petals of a dark bud opening. Konyek stood up and moved his frozen limbs, and listened to the rumbling rush of the river. The two elephants went off into the forest, but once again he waited, and watched the cows file out of the huts, the November Calf amongst them.

Now he could no longer stand the waiting, nor the endless nights alone in the forest either, and he determined to try and cross the river.

Breaking a long, stout branch from a tree, he placed it in the water to test its depth. Then he took his first step. Again he placed the stick in front of him to test the depth, and then he took his second step. In this fashion, he took one more, and yet another, until the muddy water swirled about him, and was waist deep. The current was strong, and suddenly the stick was swept away from him, and he lost his balance. He could not swim, and he cried out in terror as the current swirled him downstream, helpless as a leaf in a whirlwind. He thought he must drown, for now he was out of his depth and the water rushed in a foaming torrent about him. But just then a big log sailed by him, and he grasped on to it with all his strength. For some time he was carried along, clinging desperately to the log, and shutting his eyes tight when it seemed it must collide with a tree in the middle of the flood water.

At last the current slowed, and the river grew calmer, so that he was able to pull himself on to the log and sit astride it. Here the river was very wide, even before the flood it had been wide, and the water had reached the level of its steep banks. Now he found himself in the midst of a school of hippopotamus, no more than their small pointed ears and wicked little eyes betraying their presence. Then one leapt upwards, blowing sparkling sprays of water from its nostrils, playfully plunging and frolicking, its calf swimming beside it. When it submerged itself completely, Konyek feared the log might sail over a concealed form, and the animal cause his raft to capsize. But the hippopotamus let him pass.

The current carried him helplessly on, and suddenly he saw that there were rapids ahead. Now the log began to slip faster over the water, nearer and nearer the rushing cascades it sped until it was almost upon them, and their thunderous clamour filled his head. He shut his eyes in terror and clung to the log; then he felt himself hurled at great speed down a steep drop, racing giddily through space in a bottomless, roaring world. Then the whirling water at the foot of the cascades caught the log and flung it against the river bank. He was pitched into the mud, breathless and dazed. A crocodile watched him with eyes more wicked than the hippopotamus, and he got up, and climbed up the bank. It was good to feel the earth firm once more beneath his feet; and then he realized he was on the same side of the river as the village!

On this side of the river the slope was unforested and there were no bushes in which he could conceal himself. So he waited until dusk, and then crept past the village until he came to a solitary fig tree the other side of it. It was old, and its branches spread wide, and its trunk was stout and gnarled. There was a large hollow in the trunk, and he climbed inside this, and when more rain came, he once again waited for the new day, dry in the hollow of the tree. He listened to the wind in the leaves, and he listened to the patter of raindrops on the earth, and he fell into a light sleep. Vervet monkeys swinging in the branches ran down to peep at him, and a tiny bushbaby with a curly tail and enormous eyes that shone like polished copper in the dark. Konyek dreamed that he was riding on the back of one of the two elephants he had met in the forest, and they were making their way through tall golden grass which gleamed round them like the ripples of a golden pool, all the way to the horizon . . . He awoke, and the night was black, and he was cold and cramped.

At last the sky lightened and soon the cows began to leave the village. He saw the two herdsboys drive them up the slope of the hill, as before, and he waited until they had disappeared over the rim. Then, his heart beating quickly, he climbed the hill also, and began to follow them.

Keeping himself concealed behind bushes and trees, he followed them for half of that day, until they were at the furthest point from the village they would reach, and could not run back and get help. Then he waited until the two boys had separated so that he would not have to fight them both at once. And all the time his eyes were on the black calf, and he could hardly restrain himself.

At last the time seemed right, and his body grew taut with fearful excitement as he prepared to attack the older of the two boys. He did not doubt that he could run faster, but the boy was tall, and looked strong.

Suddenly he raced forward, swift as a cheetah and even more graceful, so that he was upon the boy almost before he saw him. He was strong indeed, but Konyek had to win the fight, because of the calf, and because he could not return without her. And so he fought with a wild fierceness, until at length he beat his foe, and the boy lay unconscious upon the ground. Then he looked round for the youth's brother, and saw that he was running in the direction of the village for help. Konyek raced after him, and caught up with him, and the boy grabbed a handful of grass to show his defeat. Then Konyek bound his hands and feet with the vines he had cut in the forest, and the hands and feet of the other boy as well. One by one he carried them into the bushes, so that they should not be found too quickly, and he would be far away if the warriors decided to give chase. Then at last he was free to go to the calf.

He strode over to her, and, slipping his arms about her neck, murmured words of joy. And the calf nuzzled him, and regarded him with her soft gaze, and his heart overflowed with happiness. When he went away from the herd, she followed him without coaxing, remaining close by his side. And so they set off together on their homeward journey.

12

The Escape

Now they had to make haste, and Konyek urged the heifer to a trot. He prayed that the two boys would not be found until the sun was low in the sky, so that if the warriors gave chase, it would not be until nightfall; then the imprints of the calf's hoofs, and of his own feet, would be concealed by the darkness. For during these nights of rain there was no moon.

Late that afternoon he crossed back into the territory of his own people, and soon he met with a herdsboy. He walked with him, so that the tracks of the calf and the tracks of his own feet mingled with those of the cattle; and now, if he were followed, his pursuers would have difficulty in picking up the trail again.

The boy invited him back to the manyatta, and offered him shelter and hospitality, for he too was of the age-group of the Big Ostrich Feathers; and so he treated Konyek as a brother. Konyek glanced longingly in the direction of the manyatta, for he would dearly have loved to spend the night in the warmth and safety of one of the huts. But he refused, because he wished to travel as far as possible before nightfall.

He took his leave of the herdsboy, and now he came to a great plain. There were scattered bushes and slender thorn trees, but there was no place he could hide; and he was clearly visible from the high ledge behind him from which he had descended into the plain. He spoke encouraging words to the calf, and patted its soft black neck, and hurried it forward as fast as he could. Because of the rain, the earth here was marshy, and slowed their steps. Often he turned his head to see if he were being followed; but all he saw was sunlight, and space, and scattered thorn trees, whose slender trunks glowed in the setting sun.

At last, he reached the other side of the wide valley, and the foot of the hills that bordered it. Just then, he looked back; and in the last rays of sunlight, he saw the glint of spears on the slope that dropped into the plain.

He felt the panic sweep over him, driving all thought from his mind; but he fought to calm himself, asking himself fiercely: "Am I a reed buck which is hypnotized by the yellow eyes of a lion?" And he tried to think what he should do, and how Ol-Poruo, his grandfather, would expect him to behave.

Without the calf, he could run swiftly, swifter than the warriors who must keep watch for his tracks. Soon it would be night, and if there were no moon, the darkness would cover his trail. Now his mind began to work rapidly and clearly, and, taking a piece of the vine that remained, he bound the forelegs of the calf. Then he raised one of her back legs and pushed her hard, so that she toppled over into the bushes. Now he bound her hind legs, and, quickly cutting branches with his knife, covered her with them so that she was concealed. Then he doubled back along the route that he had been following, taking care to cover the tracks of the calf with his own. Later he branched off in a different direction, up into the hills, praying that the new trail he was making would distract the warriors from the one which led to the calf.

The slope was steep, and it had grown dark. Clouds hurried across the sky, but sometimes the moon slipped between them and lit the land with her light. And then Konyek was full of fear that the warriors might discern the tracks of the calf, and find her.

He feared as well the devils his grandmother had told him about, and that he might meet one in the rain and in the dark. They were half man, and half lion, and they would call out to passers-by and beg them to help carry a bundle of wood. If the passer-by were foolish enough to stop, the devil would kill him with a pointed stick and devour him. Once such a devil had killed and devoured the inhabitants of a whole village, save for one woman and her son who had run away and hidden in a cave. When the boy grew up, Konyek's grandmother had said, he made bows and arrows, and the arrows he poisoned. One day, the devil saw smoke coming from the fire the boy had lighted, and came to eat him. But the boy was waiting for him, concealed in a tree, and shot the arrows at him. At first the devil thought he had been stung by gadflies, but when he was dying, he gave the boy secret directions how to recover the people of the village he had killed, and all their cattle as well. And in their gratitude, when the villagers came to life again, they elected the boy as chief.

The cunning and the bravery of the boy made Konyek ashamed of his fears, and it made him long as well for the praise of his grandfather Ol-Poruo, and of his family, and all of his age-group, if he arrived home safely with the November Calf. He did not tremble any more when the moon appeared, but carried on swiftly.

Suddenly a wind arose, and great black clouds gathered over the plain. And even as he paused and looked up at the sky, Konyek felt the first drops of rain. His body was weak with relief, and he fell down on the grass, and laughed with joy. For now all the tracks would be wiped away.

It rained as he did not remember seeing it rain before. The heavens emptied their water upon the earth, and the water began rushing down from the higher slopes into the plain. Konyek knew that in the morning it would be flooded, and he was full of anxiety for the calf. For she was unable to stand, and might drown in the water that was gathering at the foot of the hills. He forgot that he was tired, and he forgot that he was chilled and soaked, and, turning round, he hurried back.

When he came to the foot of the hills, he found that already the water was rising. Splashing through it, he called the calf's name.

Suddenly ahead of him loomed a great form, which he sensed was there even before he was able to see it. Then he saw a second form, almost the same, and even in the darkness he was quite certain that it was the two elephants he had encountered in the forest. Then he found that they were standing either side of the calf of the November Cloud, as though they were protecting her.

He slipped between the two great animals and knelt by the side of the calf. Patting her flanks, he undid the vines, and she struggled to her feet. All this time, the two elephants stood either side of him, less than an arm's length away. And although he knew they could have killed the calf or himself by moving one huge foot, he was certain that they would not do this, not even without meaning to. For he had seen the careful gentleness with which they treated their own babies. Instead of fear, he felt a safety in the presence of the two great beasts.

Now the water was rushing down the hillsides, sweeping over ledges, filling hollows and rivers until they overflowed their banks. He wanted to climb to a higher spot, but the calf was strangely reluctant to move on.

He coaxed and entreated her, but she did not respond; not even when he tried to pull her, or to push, would she move. Finally she simply lay down, and he knew then that she was sick.

The water was rising, and if she remained in that

place, she must surely drown. He struggled to carry her, but she was now much too heavy. And so he began to cut branches, and placed them first beneath her head and her neck so that he might raise her body. But he knew in his heart that even if it ceased raining, the water from the higher slopes was streaming downwards so fast, he could not save her life in this way.

Then he witnessed a wonderful thing. The two elephants prodded the calf gently on either side with their trunks, as they would a calf of their own, until they had raised her to her feet. And then they went forward, as though they understood full well the dangers of remaining in this place, supporting her between them.

And thus the strange quartet continued, until they were safely above the level of the water.

The rain ceased, day broke, and in the first smoky-grey light Konyek saw that the plain was turning into a great lake. He saw too that they were on the slope of a hill, and that on this side, its foot was surrounded by water which would soon be joined to the water of the plain.

He knew that he might be marooned on the hill, and, leaving the calf of the November Cloud in the care of the two elephants, he began to make preparations accordingly.

13

The Hill of Refuge

There was grass on the hill, and scattered bushes, and there was also a forest. Konyek went directly to this forest and cut branches to build a shelter for himself, and for the sick calf. He worked quickly, for he wanted to dry the wood, and the foliage which he would use for bedding, whilst the sun was shining. When the framework was completed, he plastered it with buffalo dung which he found nearby, so that it might be waterproof; and then he lit a fire inside, so that the heat of the flames within, and the heat of the sun without, might dry the refuge before night.

When the shadows began to lower themselves, all the work was finished; and he was exhausted, and he was hungry, for he had neither slept nor rested for two days and a night. But now he must try to coax the calf into the shelter.

She was lying on her side in the sunshine, and the two elephants were feeding close by. Then he saw one of them take a tuft of grass in its trunk, and try to feed it to her; and his heart filled with gratitude to the two great beasts.

He knelt by the calf, and stroked her neck, and managed to coax her to her feet. She began to graze then, and it seemed to him that she was a little better, and he stayed beside her; later she went with him to the shelter, and seemed content to remain there for the night.

Before the hour when the cattle return to the manyatta, he went out to the elephants. Speaking to them softly, he told them of his gratitude, for he knew no other repayment he could make them. And they looked at him with little eyes so full of kindness and wisdom, it seemed to him that perhaps they understood him.

Night gathered its dark folds about the hill and he returned to the shelter. Sinking down on the bed of leafy branches, he slept immediately. Outside, the clouds gathered, and the heavens emptied their water upon the earth again. All night long the deluge continued, but Konyek slept safe and dry, his head on the flank of the November Calf. The two elephants, undisturbed by the water streaming off their hides, kept guard.

In the morning it was still raining, and it rained all that day, and all that night, and for two more days and nights afterwards. During this time, the calf grew stronger, and began to go outside to graze. Konyek went outside also, for he was hungry and had nothing to eat. He wished the little hunter were there to help him, for he did not know in which places to seek out the berries and the roots.

His people neither tilled the soil nor gathered its harvest; they considered such work beneath them, and looked down upon those who sowed and reaped in order to live. Next to courage they prized their freedom, and it seemed to them that the farmers were chained to the earth even as a woman's bracelets were chained to her wrists.

He began his first explorations of the hill, but he could not search far because of the rain. In the forest, where the tall podo grew, and the pine, he discovered berries, and a certain nut that was sweet and nourishing. In a small clearing he found a deep pool like a secret eye of the forest; a great red-billed stork spread wide grey wings, disturbing the silence and startling him.

On his way back, he saw two hyenas watching him. He feared the hyena, for sometimes they would attack a full-grown zebra, or a wildebeest, and if sometimes they ran away, sometimes they stayed to fight as well. Best of all, they loved to seize the new-born calves at the moment of their birth, and at night, when he lay listening to their wild laugh, Konyek was glad that the calf of the November Cloud was safe beside him, and he would rub his head against her flank where it rested.

The next day, the rain slackened. He saw the vultures circling and thought there had been a kill. But instead he found an eland that had just died, perhaps of old age. Quickly, before the hyenas came, he cut strips of its hide that he might make them into thongs in case he should need them. Even as he walked away, the hyenas rushed in, and began devouring the animal. The vultures wheeled, and circled, and waited.

By the fifth day, the black calf was much stronger, the rain had stopped, and she grazed from morning until evening by the side of the two elephants. Placing his trust in them, Konyek left them to guard her. Now, for the first time, he climbed to the summit of the hill, which was high and rounded, and crowned with rocks and trees. Hummocks and dips clung to its lower slopes like knobbly knuckles, and he hunted amongst them for food; but he found nothing save the green grass and the wild flowers that had come with the rain. The flowers were small and delicately formed, and there was a fresh, sweet scent in the air, and the clear call of the birds. He climbed higher, until he came to the boulders and massive outcrops of rock. Turning to look down beneath him, he was astonished at the change that had taken place.

On one side, the plain had become a vast lake, and on the other, all the hills he could see seemed to be floating in a calm grey sea. And because each was cut off from the other by the water, it seemed to him that only the birds could make their way from summit to summit. From where he stood, he could not see any life other than the birds. The world seemed so deserted, he thought that perhaps this was as it had been when God began to prepare the earth.

He roamed amongst the rocks and the trees, then crossed the summit of the hill and descended the other side. Here the bushes grew more closely together, and he searched amongst them hungrily for berries. Suddenly he came upon a track and he felt a surge of hope, for tracks frequently led to villages.

He followed the track down the hillside, and as he drew nearer to the water's edge, he noticed brown humps like the back of a hippopotamus showing above the surface. He realized then that the path did indeed lead to a manyatta, and that the manyatta was in the valley, but the valley had been flooded and the people had fled away. Hungry and low in spirit, he turned to go back.

Just then he heard the bleating of a goat, and the bleating was repeated and distressed. The sound came from near the water's edge, and he turned back towards the foot of the hill and made his way to the place from which the sound came. Soon he saw the goat. It was stuck fast in the mud, and so was its small white kid which had almost been sucked under. He knew he must act quickly if he were to save the animals, but he did not dare approach nearer unless he too sank into the mire. And so, quickly as he could, he began to hack branches from the bushes, and with the branches he made a pathway across the treacherous mud. All the time he could see the goat struggling, and sinking a little deeper into the mire; and now the small head of the kid began to disappear. He placed the last branch in front of him and took one more careful step forward; then reaching down pulled the small form from the sucking grasp of the mud and laid it on the pathway of wood. Then he tied one of the leather thongs he had made from the eland skin round the neck of the struggling goat, and began dragging it to safety. When at last he had hauled it on to the branches, he picked up the kid and led the goat away from the mire.

As soon as they were back on firm earth, he cleaned the mud off the still form of the kid, and tried to massage the water out of it, and warmed its tiny body with his hands. Then, holding it close to the warmth of his own body, and leading the goat by the leather strap, he turned his steps homewards.

He had not been away so long before, and he was anxious about the calf of the November Cloud. But when he got back, he found her grazing safely beside the two elephants.

Tethering the goat to a tree, he went into his refuge and lit a fire, and sat nursing the kid in his arms. It was still alive, but it was very sick and he did not know if it would live till morning. He laid it on his bed of leafy branches, and went to fetch the goat. For a while he had forgotten his hunger, absorbed in the task of rescuing the animals; but now it had returned, and he saw that the udders of the goat were full. He milked them straight into his mouth, and the taste was wonderfully sweet and satisfying; it was a long time since a drop of milk had passed his lips and warmed his hollow stomach. But he only half-emptied the goat's udders so that there might be sufficient for the kid should she recover. He got up from the ground and took the goat into the shelter, and the November Calf as well.

Now it was dark, and he lay down to sleep, and did not waken till first light. And when he did, he heard a strange sound which at first he could not place – until he realized it was the sound of the kid suckling. Then he was filled with happiness because the kid was alive. And he was happy, too, because now he had a goat, and would not again feel hungry high on this hill where he must stay until the flood water subsided.

14

The Elephants Save the November Calf

The days passed, the rain continued to fall and the flood water to rise. Konyek extended his refuge so that the goat and kid might have a place of their own to sleep at night, cutting a small opening so that he might crawl from his part of the shelter into that of the goats. Often he felt a great wave of longing for his home and his family, and he wondered how much time must pass before he could return to them. He wondered as well whether they would ever believe his story, for even had Parmet not lied to them, it would be a strange tale that he had to tell. But he was not unhappy, for he had a warm place to sleep at night, and milk to drink, and the company of the animals – the November Calf especially.

The two elephants remained with him, and he was grateful for their presence. Each morning when he arose, he looked to see if they were still there, because he knew of the comings and goings of the elephant, and their inexplicable journeying. Sometimes they would disappear round a curve of the hill, or be hidden in a dip, and he would hurry off in search of them, afraid that they had wandered away and would never come back. But he always found them. And usually not far from his refuge, so that he felt that they kept guard over his home by night, and his calf by day.

One morning, perhaps two weeks after he had come to the hill, he set out to search the slope on the side that faced towards the east. It was rockier here, and there were caves where many bats dwelt. Hyrax scuttled past him, and he had seen, too, the spoor of a leopard. There was a little sunshine that morning, and he lingered in its warmth near a herd of gazelles with fawn coats and black stripes on their flanks. Suddenly the two males charged one another, locking their delicately wrought horns as they met and fighting viciously. The females stood close by, watching with Konyek. After a while, he rushed in on them, and they unlocked their horns and fled away, the females in their wake. Now he turned towards home.

When he came to the slope where he had built his refuge, he heard a frantic barking and braying. Then he saw a herd of zebra racing in a frenzied circle which broke into a stream of striped bodies as the creatures fled across the hillside. Behind them raced the hyena, and the one in the lead was just within reach of the hindmost zebra. Four others were running close behind it, and if once he caught the animal's tail in his teeth, the others would close in and force it to the ground and tear it to pieces.

Konyek gave hardly a thought to the zebra, because near them was the calf of the November Cloud. And for once, the two elephants were nowhere to be seen. He began to race towards her, and at that moment, the hindmost zebra suddenly turned and bit the hyena, so that with a yelp of pain he gave up the attack. Now the pack turned their attention to the helpless calf, and swerving round, made towards her.

Konyek saw her standing there, too dazed with terror to move. Faster he ran, and yet faster, but it seemed to him that he was no closer to her, as in a nightmare. Then he heard a great trumpeting, and from round a curve in the hill-slope there appeared the two elephants. They tossed their heads and flapped their great ears in anger and charged straight at the hyena; and now the hyena were as full of fear as the calf, and ran away until they had disappeared from sight. Konyek felt his body grow weak with relief. The two elephants had saved the life of his calf, and his heart was full. Then the female touched the calf with her trunk, as she would a baby of her own; he had never seen her do that before. From that day on he called the female elephant Yoyo, which is Masai for mother, and the male Leng-aina which is Masai for "of the Long Arm", and means elephant as well. And now that the two elephants had names, they were distinguished from all other elephants, and he thought of them as friends.

The following morning, when he got up and went outside, he could not find Yoyo and Leng-aina anywhere. He looked for them below the shelter and above it; he looked eastwards and westwards, and he called to them as well. But still they did not appear. He searched further, but it had rained in the night, and the rain had washed out their tracks, so that first he grew alarmed, and then sad. The hill seemed lonely and unprotected without them.

He had shut the goat and her kid in the shelter, blocking the entrance with large stones; but the November Calf he had taken with him. Now he stood very still beside her, listening and concentrating intently for some sign of the elephants. It seemed to him that everything else, the bushes and the trees, the grass and even the very earth, was strangely still as well. And he had a feeling that something very special was happening, and the feeling was like a vibrant stillness that he could not explain. Yet he was certain that the trees and the bushes, and the grass under his feet, all knew of this thing; perhaps even the November Calf too.

For some time he remained where he was, listening and concentrating intently. The herd of zebra grazed not far away, and two chestnut impala; a honey-bird called, but he did not heed it. Then, as though pulled in that direction by a strange force, he began to descend the hill towards a clump of trees. He walked through the thicket and found himself on a ledge that followed the curve of the slope. A little further on the ledge gentled and there were tall bushes and long grass. Here he came upon

Yoyo and Leng-aina.

Yoyo lifted her head and trumpeted warningly, and he stood still, surprised, for this had never happened before. Then Leng-aina moved to one side, so that he was no longer partially concealing Yoyo. And then Konyek saw what had happened, and he was filled with wonder and excitement.

15

The Birth of Ol-Kulto

Beneath Yoyo there lay a newborn calf, a perfect miniature of her huge self. She nudged it to its feet with her trunk, and Konyek saw that it had been washed clean by the rain; then he saw the vultures circling, waiting to devour the afterbirth. The baby was unsteady on its feet, and already it began to search for its mother's milk. But it was searching between its mother's hind legs instead of her front ones, and it was so weak it toppled over again. Its mother helped it up once more, and again the search began for milk; but even when it found her breast, it had to reach so high with its trunk in order to suckle, the effort was too much for it, and it fell back upon the grass. The mother walked a few paces forward, then turned and nudged the calf on to its feet, which were so new they were still quite tender.

Konyek sat down and watched this struggle to begin life; the struggle to stand, and the struggle to reach the life-giving milk. But the mother was patient and gentle, and caressed the small animal with her trunk as a woman might caress a baby with her hand, until finally it succeeded, and began to suckle.

All that day Konyek remained nearby, with the calf of the November Cloud. He wondered about the moment when the two calves met one another, and whether they would be friends. He decided to give the new calf a name, even as the calves in his father's herd were named when they were born. And because for the past two weeks every night the heavens had emptied their water upon the earth, at first he called it the Calf of the Great Storms. But as he sat there watching it and marvelling at its smallness, he found himself calling it affectionately Ol-Kulto, which is Masai for caterpillar, but one that is very weak and very small.

This name pleased him as well because it reminded him of the story of the caterpillar his grandmother had told him:

Once there was a caterpillar who went to live in the home of a hare. When the hare returned home, she saw the footprints and called out:

"Who is in my hut?"

And the caterpillar replied in a great voice: "I am the warrior of the Lone One who fought so bravely at the battle of Kurtiale. I crushed the rhinoceros to the earth! I made cow's dung of the elephant! I am invincible!"

The hare was quite astounded, and did not dare try to enter her home, and hurried off to tell the other animals. First she told the hyena, who laughed and laughed, and would not believe the story. But the hare begged the hyena to go to her house and see for himself. And so the hyena went, and standing outside the home of the hare cried out in a great voice:

"Tell me who is within!"

And the caterpillar replied in a still greater voice: "I am the warrior of the Lone One who fought so bravely at the battle of Kurtiale. I crushed the rhinoceros to the earth! I made cow's dung of the elephant! I am invincible!"

Whereupon the hyena put his tail between his legs and ran off.

Now the hare went to the rhinoceros and told him her story, and the rhinoceros snorted irritably, and he too refused to believe her words. But she persuaded him to go and see for himself, and the rhinoceros went to her home and, standing outside, called in a mighty voice:

"I am the fierce rhinoceros. Who has dared to enter the home of the hare?"

And the caterpillar replied with the same words as before, in a mightier voice: "I am the warrior of the Lone One who fought so bravely at the battle of Kurtiale! I crushed the rhinoceros to the earth! I made cow's dung of the elephant! *I am invincible*!"

Whereupon the rhinoceros was astonished, and had no words, and trotted back into the bushes from which he had come.

By now all the animals had heard the story and each of them went to the house of the hare, and stood outside, and called in a great voice: "Who is within?" And to each of them the caterpillar replied in a voice yet greater: "I am the warrior of the Lone One!" Even the leopard went, and the lion, and finally the elephant, who is the mightiest of them all. And when the caterpillar heard the heavy tread of the elephant that makes the earth shake, and heard his rumbling voice, he was full of terror. But he hid his fear and replied in the same mighty voice:

"I am the warrior of the Lone One who fought so bravely at the battle of Kurtiale! I crushed the rhinoceros to the earth! I made cow's dung of the elephant! *I am invincible*!" Whereupon even the elephant was afraid, and went away.

Of all the animals only the frog had not yet visited the house of the hare, and now at last he made his way there. And when he arrived he stood outside and said in a scornful tone:

"I am the strong person, the leaper, and I have buttocks like a post, and God has made me vile!"

Upon which the caterpillar trembled and said in a small voice:

"I am only the caterpillar."

Then all the animals laughed because the tiny caterpillar had fooled even the strongest and the largest of them.

And so now, looking at the tiny calf to which the mighty Yoyo had given birth, it seemed to Konyek that little caterpillar, Ol-Kulto, was a fitting name for it; and that when it grew older he could call it the Calf of the Great Storms.

16

The Departure from the Hill

For a few days, Konyek continued to stay a short distance away from Ol-Kulto and his mother. He knew how nervous the elephants were when their babies were born, and how carefully they guarded them. But the small elephant was curious, and after a while, he came over to the November Calf and touched her with his sensitive little trunk that he might get to know her. Then he tried to put the tip of his trunk into her mouth, in the affectionate manner of elephants when they greet one another. And from that moment, the two calves were always together.

Ol-Kulto quickly became attached to Konyek as well. When his mother grew less nervous, and guarded him less zealously, he even followed Konyek into the shelter, feeling the walls of branches with his trunk until it was all familiar. He was very playful, and liked to chase after Konyek in the fashion of a child, and he was affectionate in the way of a child as well, so that Konyek began to feel towards him as he felt towards the November Calf. Soon Yoyo came to trust Konyek fully, and even while her calf was feeding, let him come close.

The white kid, too, was playful. It skipped and leapt around Ol-Kulto, who was not nearly so nimble. Often he tripped and tumbled in their games together, and this made Konyek laugh. Ol-Kulto loved to play in the water as well, and when Yoyo and Leng-aina dug muddy wallows so that they might roll in the soft, cool earth, this delighted the small elephant most of all. Often he sheltered beneath the stomach of his mother, in the dark, safe place between her four massive legs; but Yoyo never trod on her tiny calf, despite the great size of her feet.

Each day Ol-Kulto grew stronger, and each day Konyek became a little more familiar with the unceasing activity on this hill where he lived. White egrets followed in the footsteps of the elephants, eating the insects that they unearthed with each step of their great feet; and a family of mongoose lived close to the refuge, in an empty anthill almost as tall as the calf. Often Konyek would see two ostriches, and one day he found the male courting the female. Its magnificent black and white plumage spread in a great fan, it bowed gracefully to the ground, and swayed on its long legs as the foliage of a tree sways on its trunk in the wind. And it seemed to him, as he stood watching, that his people had named the ostrich well, for they called it *sidai*, which is Masai for beautiful.

Often he watched the baboons playing, the

babies riding on their mothers' backs, and sometimes a herd of graceful impala joined the baboons in their games on the hill. Sometimes, when the rain ceased and the moon struggled through the clouds for a brief while, he liked to slip out at night. The great elephants trod so silently, he would smell them, or catch sight of their grey silhouettes even before he had heard them. He had seen jackals slip past in the silvery darkness of the night, and once he had looked into the yellow eyes of a lion. But he had stood motionless, and it had continued on its way, taking no notice of him.

Now that he could leave the November Calf safely with the two elephants, he would roam for hours in the forest. By the secret pool whose water lay still and pale as a seed pearl in an oyster-bed, he would watch the tall stork feed. Touracos with scarlet wings flashed through the leaves like flames, and there were many butterflies whose colours were like the colours of the sky when the sun rises, and also when it sets.

Sometimes, when he returned to the refuge, it would be almost dusk, and it would seem to him that the three elephants and the November Calf were waiting for him; and the goat and her kid as well. Often his thoughts turned to his home and his family, and yet though he longed to be with them again, he was not unhappy.

There came a day when no rain fell, this was followed by another, and another. Konyek knew then that the black god had wrung the last drop of water from the clouds, and the heavens would empty no more water upon the earth for a long while to come. He climbed to the summit of the hill, and looking down he saw that at last the flood water was lowering itself, and soon he would be able to leave the hill. And he thought of his mother and his father, and his brother and sisters, and he thought of his grandmother and Ol-Poruo, and he was glad. Then he thought of Parmet, and he was afraid. When he returned back down the hill, he saw the cow calf and the elephant calf caught in a golden web of evening light, and he was sad. For he knew that a time would soon come when he must part from his friends the elephants, and when the November Calf must part from them, too.

Now each day the new strength of the sun began to dry the water, and it seemed to Konyek that the elephants were growing restless. Soon they would be able to continue their wanderings, and to search for the rest of the herd as he must search for his family. And one morning, when he got up, they were gone.

He searched for them, and he called, but he knew that he would not find them. Perhaps they had waited for him as long as they could, until at last, driven by some instinct deep within them, they had had to move on. He was filled with sadness, and he saw too that the November Calf pined for Ol-Kulto. And he was sad because he was alone, just as all men are sad when they live alone; yet he knew he would be happy when he returned to his family just as the calf would be happy when she was back with the herd. And so that very day, picking up his knife and his stick and his thongs of eland hide, and taking with him the goat and the kid and the November Calf, he set off on his journey home.

When he reached the bottom of the hill, he turned to look back. For a long time he gazed at the dips and the hollows, at the trees and the bushes, and the hummocks and the mounds that clustered round the summit like green knuckles. For he wanted never to forget them; he did not know if he would ever come back, and the face of the hill was as the face of a friend. So now he gave it a name, and called it the Hill of Good Refuge. He had found shelter and nourishment there, and its slopes had sheltered and nourished as well the November Calf, the goats and the three elephants. At last he turned away, and began to cross the valley.

17

The Journey Home

The mud was thick, and sometimes they waded through pools of water, so that at first they progressed slowly. But then they left the valley, and trod upon higher land, and the way became easier. When dusk fell, Konyek tethered the goat to a thorn tree, and he slept as he had so often slept, with his head upon the flank of the November Calf. But his dreams were troubled with visions of Parmet, and always Parmet was chasing him with a silver spear in his hand while the rest of the boys of the age-group of the Big Ostrich Feathers stood by and laughed; and the girls as well. But in the morning when he woke, he saw that all the land was golden and green, and the rivers laughed with water, and the sky was bluer than the petals of the wild columbine, and he forgot his dreams.

Later that day, an old man fell in step beside him, and asked him whence he came, and whither he was bound. Konyek told him then of the attack by the raiders, of the way in which he had been saved by the little hunter, and how the hunter had taken him to the village of the raiders; and how, in the end, he had retrieved the calf. Then the old man said:

"I know the Dorobo of whom you speak. I passed by the place where you were lying wounded, and he asked me to tell your people where you were, and what had happened to you. But when I came to your village, the people had already left, and started on their way to another place higher in the hills where there was still a little water for the cattle."

Then Konyek asked: "Know you to which place they went?"

"They took the road that leads past the dry lake bed – although it is full of water now – and then they went through the forest where the tall cedars and the podo grow. After that they crossed the hills that are called the hills of the Seven Oxen, because they have seven humps in the manner of our cattle, and somewhere on the next range of hills they have settled. When you approach nearer, you must enquire once more. But everyone knows the dwelling place of Ol-Poruo of the Unconquered Shield, Ol-Poruo, the son of the great prophet who foresaw the coming of men with skins pale as the moon, and hair the colour of the cassia flowers."

And he looked at the boy who was the great-grandson of the prophet who was known as Ol-le-Langoi, and saw that he was tall and slender, and fair to look upon. He knew, too, that he must be brave, for he had retrieved the black calf; but now he wondered why he had stayed away so long. And when he asked Konyek, and Konyek told him how he had lived on the Hill of Good Refuge with the elephants, he half believed him and half did not. To pass the time as they walked, and to test him, the old man asked him riddles. First of all he said:

"What do my warriors resemble when they stand on one leg?"

And Konyek replied without hesitation: "The euphorbia trees."

Then the old man asked: "What are my warriors like when they stand in a circle and one cannot see which is the first and which is the last?"

And Konyek replied equally as quickly: "The pegs that are used for pegging out a skin and stretching it."

Then the old man said: "What are the two skins I possess, the one I lie on, and the one which covers me?"

And Konyek answered: "The one is the earth and the other is the sky."

And finally the old man asked: "What is a strip of hide like when the tip is wet?"

And Konyek said: "The road which ends in water."

The old man nodded his head, satisfied. Now they came to the point where their paths parted, and they took their leave of one another, and went their separate ways.

That night, Konyek slept beneath a giant fig tree, and there was the wind in the leaves, and the bickering of the stream, and during the night he heard the low growling of a lion. In the morning, when he awoke, he saw a long striped snake hanging from the branches of the tree, but he sat quietly, and felt no fear, nor tried to harm it. For his people believed that when a great man died, his spirit went to heaven, but when one who was good but not great died, it passed into the body of a serpent. And he squeezed the udders of the goat between his fingers so that a little milk fell upon the ground, and this he left for the serpent. Then once again he continued on his path.

Later that day he passed through the forest of the tall cedars, and came to the hills of the Seven Oxen; and here he met with a band of boys and youths. They were singing joyously as they walked, and he knew that they were celebrating the last days of their boyhood; and that they were wandering from manyatta to manyatta in the happy time of anticipation before the great day of their circumcision. None of the boys was from his own manyatta, but they were of the age of the Big Ostrich Feathers, and so he knew that the date for the ceremony had been set, and he too would join the bands of the wanderers. Konyek felt the excitement leap within him. But then he saw that they were regarding him curiously, and that one of them was whispering to the others, suddenly recalling the story of the boy Konyek and his calf. Then the boys laughed mockingly, and went on their way, singing as they walked.

Now he was deeply troubled, and his steps dragged across the hillside, for he knew that far and wide they had heard the lies of Parmet. He walked close to the November Calf, and the soft warmth of her body comforted him a little.

At the hour when the cattle return to the manyatta, he began to climb the second range of hills. Just as he was wondering which direction to take, he heard the sound of chanting, and he smelt the smell of cattle dung, and of burning *leleshwa* wood. And he followed the sound and the smells, and a little before nightfall, he came to a manyatta.

Peering through the barrier of branches, he saw warriors dancing, springing high into the air so that their hair swept upwards as they leapt; and the women too were dancing in a group of their own, jerking their bodies rhythmically. And amongst the women he recognized his mother, and his older sister as well. His heart beat quickly, and the excitement leapt inside him again even as the warriors leapt in their dance. But then he caught sight of Parmet, and the gladness died like a small wind on a hot day.

Now he was reluctant to enter the manyatta, and remained outside, close to the calf, watching. He knew that these warriors were the first to come down from the hills where they had spent the last days of their warriorhood; soon their mothers would cut their elaborately dressed hair, and the coppery, twisted strands would fall upon the stretched cowhide on which they sat. And just as a tree loses its leaves or comes into blossom according to the season, so the men gave up their hair and passed from the season of warriorhood into the season of married men. They would leave room for a new generation of warriors, and the new warriors would leave room for a new generation of newly initiated men. For their lives followed a cycle as clearly marked as the cycles of nature, passing from childhood to age just as the seasons pass from spring to winter. And now the time was approaching when he would leave his childhood behind him and progress to the state of man. But he did not rejoice in his heart as the youths he had met on the path, for he feared the lies of his cousin Parmet. He feared as well the anger of his father, and the displeasure of his grandfather Ol-Poruo, because of the things which Parmet had said, and because he had left the manyatta without their permission.

In the bright moonlight, the people continued dancing. Now the men and women danced together, and so bright was the moon he could see the ochre shining on their bodies. Konyek felt plain and dull, because he had no ochre upon him to make him look beautiful. So he crept away and hid in the woods near the manyatta, and once again he spent the night beneath the stars beside the November Calf.

He was awakened by voices, and in the misty light that floats between night and dawn, he saw that the Elders together with the married men from the manyatta had brought an ox into the wood, and were about to slaughter it. He saw his father, and he saw Ol-Poruo, and his heart beat like a drum. Then he saw his father help tie the ox, and when it was lying on its side, another of the men crouched down and stuck a knife in the nape of its neck, killing it swiftly. The men skinned and quartered it, and others built a grill of wood. Yet others made fire, and when all was ready, they roasted the meat slowly, talking in small groups amongst themselves.

All this he watched without revealing himself. He saw, too, the women come up from the manyatta to take their share of the meat, for neither they nor the children were permitted to eat with the men. He saw his grandmother and his mother, and he wanted to call out to them, but still he waited. Then when the men began their feasting, he slipped away through the trees.

He knew that he could not conceal himself any longer, but he wanted his father and Ol-Poruo to be present in the manyatta when he entered. For he did not wish anything to pass between Parmet and himself which they did not hear. He knew that they would return to the manyatta when the feasting was over, and so he waited until the shadows began to lower themselves.

Then he went down to the manyatta.

18

The Judgement of Konyek

Konyek entered with his arm over the neck of the November Calf, and the goat followed on its lead with the white kid at its side. And as he entered, the chanting and the dancing stopped, and the people stared at him and were still. Then his father and his grandfather Ol-Poruo came forward, and his father said:

"You were away for many weeks, and we had thought that you were dead."

"Parmet left me to die in the valley when the warriors attacked and wounded me," Konyek replied. And the fierceness of his tone surprised the people as much as his appearance in the manyatta, for they knew the sweetness of his spirit, and his gentleness.

"His words are lies!" Parmet cried. "Did I not tell you that he left the herd with the black calf? If I had not spoken the truth, how is it that now he returns with his arm around its neck?"

And the people began to murmur their assent,

but Ol-Poruo silenced them, and told Konyek to relate all that had happened to him since he left. Then Konyek told them of the little hunter, and how he had helped him; he told them of the nights he had spent in the forest, and of the flooded river; he told them of his fight with the herdsboy, and how he had won back the calf of the November Cloud. He described the pursuit of the warriors, and the storm when it broke, and he told them of Yoyo and Lengaina and how the two elephants had stayed with him on the Hill of Good Refuge. But before he had come to the end of his tale, Parmet began to laugh, and his laughter was loud and derisive, and the rest of the boys and girls of his age-group laughed with him; and even many of the married men and women too. Then Konyek was wretched with shame and bitter with anger, and suddenly, wrenching his orange sarong from where it covered his shoulder, he pointed to the scar of his wound, which was still new. A long, deep scar it was, and the people gathered round to gaze upon it, and for a moment Parmet was confused.

"See the wound that I received from the spear of the warriors!" Konyek cried in fierce tones, "Was it there when I left the manyatta? Let him say, any man who has seen it!"

Then Parmet cried: "Prove to us that it was the spear of the enemy! You have been away a long time. Perhaps you met with a lion on your hill – or perhaps you went too close to your friends the elephants!" On hearing this the people began to

laugh once more, and this encouraged Parmet, and he shouted mockingly:

"Perhaps the crocodiles chased you along the bank of the flooded river, or maybe a hippopotamus caught you with its tooth, or maybe the herdsboy bit you when you fought with him – as you say. Yet you would have us believe it was the spear of the raiders! Was I not there, and did I not see what happened with my own eyes? Or did one of them follow you into the bushes where you had run, perhaps, and punish you for your cowardice?"

Now all the people began to talk at once, and some of them to jeer as well. But Ol-Poruo silenced them again, telling them that in the morning they would meet beneath the giant fig tree near the manyatta, so that they might judge the affair in accordance with their custom.

Parmet looked at Konyek, and the hatred was in his eyes; Ol-Poruo's gaze and the gaze of his father were stern, and his mother averted her eyes. His brother Marangu's glance was anxious and uncertain, and only the little children looked upon him as they had looked upon him before.

All the people went into their huts, but Konyek remained without. He stood beside the November Calf, and it seemed to him that she was his only friend.

The moon came up, and once again he slept beside the calf, and again he was troubled by dreams of Parmet. Long before daylight he awoke, shivering with cold, but he would not go into his hut. He watched the gleaming summit of Kilimanjaro which for so long had been hidden by the rain and the clouds, and it looked to him as beautiful as a silver ostrich egg which some giant ostrich had laid upon the clouds. Then he thought of the approaching meeting beneath the giant fig tree, and his heart was heavy because he had no means to prove his story.

Before the hour when the sun adorns the sky, he slipped out of the manyatta, so that he would not have to face the women when they appeared to milk the cows. He took the goat and the kid and the calf of the November Cloud, and let them graze near the fig tree.

Soon the people began to approach – in twos and threes they came – and they sat beneath the tree in a wide semi-circle at the feet of the Elders. When all were assembled, one of the Elders picked up the spokesman's horn and addressed the people. Then he summoned Konyek before him.

Once again he told his story, but this time the Elders questioned every detail, examining them one by one as a witch-doctor examines the magic stones in his gourd, and chewing them with great thoroughness as a cow chews the cud. They asked him as well why he had not returned to the manyatta before going in search of the calf; upon which he told them of the old man, and the message given to him by the hunter. But they did not believe this, for no old man had come. Nor did they believe he had met the Elder on his journey home, when the old man had said that he had indeed been to the manyatta, but the people had departed. And they all agreed he should have returned to the manayatta, and he should not have set out on his own without the permission of his father.

Parmet too was questioned, and again he told how Konyek had gone to rest in the shade of the bushes, taking the black calf with him. Then he, Parmet, had heard the cries of the warriors, and he had tried to force the cattle to run off into the bushes and scatter Konyek's as well. And he had called to his cousin to come and help him, but Konyek had not answered, and had run deeper into the bushes with the black calf.

Then the Elders discussed Parmet's story, and Konyek's, and they passed the facts to and fro like a woman weaving the threads of a basket. All day they talked and argued, until the sun slipped behind the hills, and all that was left of its fire was a trail of golden smoke. At last the Elders agreed that Parmet must be telling the truth, because had not Konyek returned with the black calf, even as he had disappeared into the bushes with it? And who amongst them had heard of a man living with elephants? A Masai lived with his cattle, and with other men such as themselves. And then again, he should not have gone away from the manyatta, on his own, without first seeking the permission of his elders. The people murmured their assent, and Konyek saw that his father's face was stern, and ashamed, and he felt the shame in himself, and the hopelessness. But he felt the fierceness of his anger as well when he heard his cousin's loud laughter and saw the spite in his eyes, and the triumph. When he looked at his grandfather, Ol-Poruo, he saw nothing in his face at all, for it was as a mask.

The Elders adjourned the meeting until the following day, when it would be decided the manner in which Konyek should be punished. But already the girls and boys of his age-group refused to speak with him, and taunted him with mocking words when they did. Konyek turned suddenly, and strode swiftly away from them with the calf of the November Cloud, and found a place where he could sit by himself. His smallest brothers and sisters, who did not understand all that had occurred, found him there, and were full of gladness at his return. They believed his stories of Yoyo and Leng-aina, and asked him to tell them again and again. And as they sat together, the smallest one on his lap, the stillness was shattered by a sudden wild trumpeting, which was the trumpeting of an elephant in pain. Immediately, although he could not tell why, Konyek knew that it was Yoyo and Leng-aina. Swiftly he ran off to find them, while the children went back into the manyatta, as he commanded. They told the others where Konyek had gone, and the men and the boys followed him.

When they caught sight of him, they stopped in fear and amazement, for they saw a strange and astonishing thing. There were three elephants, two full grown, and a small calf. One of the elephants was lying on the ground, an arrow quivering in her great flank, and the calf was beside her, anxiously touching her with its little trunk. The male elephant was standing by her side also, and he too was touching her gently and anxiously with his trunk. But Konyek was squatting on her flank, and although he was pulling the poisoned arrow from her side, she lay quite still, and did not harm him! The people stared, and were silent, and could scarcely believe their eyes. Then they heard Konyek talking gently to the animal, and they saw the small calf touch him with its trunk, and they saw that it was not afraid; rather, it seemed that it knew him.

Then another amazing thing happened. Suddenly the November Calf came rushing past them, straight up to the elephant, and the baby ran its trunk over her, and tried to put it in her mouth, and none could doubt the bond that existed between them.

Just then, a figure appeared from amongst the trees. He was small and wiry, his legs were thin and crooked as the branches of the whistling thorn, and the little eyes in his wizened face were bright with kindness, and with cunning. He called to Konyek, for he did not dare to go close to the elephants. And Konyek heard him, and jumped up, the arrow still in his hand, and ran over to him, and greeted him warmly. Then all the people heard Konyek say:

"I know full well that you and your people are hunters of elephant and eaters of elephant meat, but I beg you to spare the life of this one. She helped me, even as you helped me, and I beg you to give me some medicine that will clean the arrow's deadly poison."

Whereupon the hunter opened his leather bag,

and, taking out a small horn that was closed at one end, he took off the leather lid and told Konyek to pour some of the powder into the wound that the poison might not spread. Swiftly Konyek did as he was bid, and all the while the cow calf and the elephant calf remained close beside each other.

When Konyek had finished ministering to the elephant, Ol-Poruo summoned the hunter to him, and asked him to tell of his meeting with Konyek and all that occurred after that. Then the Dorobo told how he had found him in the valley, grievously wounded, and how he had taken him into the shelter of the bushes, and tended him until he grew well. He told, too, of the old man who had passed in the valley and how he had asked the Elder to take a message to the manyatta. And finally, when no one from the manyatta had come, how he had taken Konyek to the village of the raiders, and not set eyes upon him again until this moment.

Then all the people began to speak at once, their voices rising like the sound of rain when it beats on the ground in a storm, for they knew that Konyek had spoken the truth, and no word of his story had he invented. Silencing them, Ol-Poruo turned towards Parmet. The lines of his face were set and stern, and he commanded the youth to explain the lies he had told, and why he had left his cousin to die on the plain.

But Parmet could not. For a long while now he had been shaking with fear, and when he tried to speak, he stammered and stuttered, so that none could understand him. Then all the boys and girls of the year of the Big Ostrich Feathers turned upon him with angry words and abused him for the shameful manner in which he had acted. Again Ol-Poruo silenced them, for the matter was not yet concluded. And he said:

"It is a well-known saying amongst our people that a calf is as good as a man, for if a man guards a calf well, that calf grows into a fine cow, and that cow gives many cows of her own. Then the man becomes rich and can buy many wives and have many children. Now Konyek acted with great courage, and he retrieved the calf of the November Cloud, and she will grow into a fine cow; so that perhaps, as a reward for his courage, one day his father will give him this calf which he loves so well. To his faithful friend, the hunter who twice saved his life, we will give an ox that he might feast upon it with his kinsmen, and a cow in calf that he might have milk."

And Konyek's heart overflowed with happiness, and the girls and boys of the year of the Big Ostrich Feathers gathered round him, and sang and danced. That night, he sat in the little dwelling of earth and twigs once more, and the Dorobo came, too, and accepted a drinking horn of honey-wine. The fire-light in its circle of stones lit his mother's smiling face and the tiers of beaded necklaces that circled outwards from her neck to her shoulders; it lit the circle of children gathered round it, and his grand-mother's old face that was lined as the earth in the time of drought. It flickered as well upon the rounded calabash of milk that stood upon the ground, and the warmth and safety of the firelit room were all about him, even as a warm garment, and he was happy.

When his grandmother had told them a story, Konyek slipped outside into the moonlight, and, taking the November Calf with him, went back to see the elephants. Now he saw there were not three, but many, and that Leng-aina was standing on one side of Yoyo, and a strange elephant on the other, and that between them they had helped her to her feet. He did not approach near, because of the strange elephant, but suddenly Ol-Kulto caught wind of him, and of the November Calf, and came running over to them. The elephants began to move off, and they trumpeted angrily at Ol-Kulto, commanding him to follow. He turned and ran after them, then stopped midway between Konyek and the November Calf, and the herd. There he stood, a small animal in the moonlit space between the forest and the sloping hills; then at last he trotted uncertainly after the herd. Konyek watched him disappear into the trees, and in the midst of his happiness there was a kernel of sadness, like the hidden pool in the heart of the forest on his hill. And he knew that with all men this must be so, and that for him, his initiation had begun the day the raiders had made their attack.

All was stillness and silence now, and he returned to the manyatta with the Calf of the November Cloud whom that night, his father had given him for his own.